CW01095350

1

2

THE MISTRESS OF THE MAZE: THE LEGEND OF ROSAMUND CLIFFORD

BY

J.P. REEDMAN

The nuns of Godstow gathered in silence as the great Bishop, Hugh of Lincoln, processed through the courtyard of their humble priory. The man was said to be marked for sainthood, and as the sunbeams danced on his tall mitre and turned his white alb incandescent, he certainly seemed wreathed in holy, heavenly light.

Unfortunately, his face did not match the glory of his sun-haloed attire; his face was as sour as a withered autumn apple and as creased; the mouth tight and pursed, the skin tone grey and unhealthy from spending hours in churches upon his knees. Little, snake-like, dark eyes darted about, seeking for any improprieties he could spot in the behaviour of the nuns.

It was rumours of 'irregularities' that had caused him to descend upon Godstow with his entourage. Disturbing news of heathenish activities had reached him in his diocese, giving him sleepless nights where he tossed and turned. The nuns were worshipping inappropriately and allowing others in the region to do likewise. (That some people might consider his own behaviour improper, when he had bitten into the arm bone of St Mary Magdalen at Fecamp in an attempt to wrest it from its legitimate monkish owners, never occurred to Hugh at all. Such an action, for him, was perfectly acceptable...Why shouldn't the English church, rising in importance these last years, have Mary Magdalen's blessed arm bone for its own?)

The problem at Godstow, however, was quite different from a tug or war over a holy relic. The nuns here were frivolous women, as women were wont to be in Hugh of Lincoln's estimation...and, according to his sources, they were worshipping a whore. A whore. (He seemed to have forgotten that Mary Magdalen was rumoured to have been a whore...but that was different. Naturally.)

He would put an end to such sinfulness He had already sorted out a similar problem in the town of Northampton, where the locals were venerating a known felon's tomb in All Saints Church. The day had been hard won then, with Hugh having to leap atop a tomb and swing his crozier about like a weapon. A few heads were cracked that day, which secretly pleased him. Smiting for the Lord. However, he doubted it would be so difficult to restore order here, with only a pack of sheep-like women to tame.

4

Gesturing his party forward, Hugh walked briskly down the covered cloisters and entered the door of the priory church. As he stepped over the threshold, its pungent smell assailed his sensitive nose; he flared his nostrils out angrily, trying to discern what the heady, almost sickly fragrance belonged to. The usual aromas of tallow and incense permeated the air, but another scent lingered, mingling with the others, triumphing over them.

Suddenly he knew—roses, many roses, just as if a rosery bloomed within the nave of that holy place. For a moment, doubt claimed him; he remembered that when Our Lady appeared to perform a miracle, she was said to leave a scent of roses in her wake…but that surely could not be the case here, in this den of folly and sin. The Blessed Virgin would weep at the very thought of appearing amongst these erring nuns.

The roses he smelt were not holy; even as he sniffed again he was certain gall and wormwood tainted their odour….Tainted them with sin itself.

Scowling, he shuffled up the nave, under the soaring chancel arch and into the choir of the church. There, before the high altar, stood a solitary chest-tomb. Not a very large tomb, but ornate, covered in decorated panels—it had clearly cost someone a great deal of money. Wreaths of flowers covered the tomb's surface, some wildflowers but mainly roses—roses in red, roses in white, some fresh, newly plucked from the bush, others decayed, the rims of their sagging petals withered and black. Candles of all shapes and sizes stood between the wreaths, glowing and flickering in the breeze from the now-open door. Tallow ran in thick yellow ropes over the marble top, while coloured light streamed through the painted glass windows on either side of the adjacent altar, dappling the warm sandstone of the chest with its fading traces of paint. Carved Fleur de Lys, lions, giants, a chalice almost like a communion cup, and roses in unholy disarray snarled together amidst decorations of stone thorns.

An irrational anger flared up in Bishop Hugh's breast at the sight of the tomb and its carvings and offerings. Righteous anger, delivered straight from God, of that he was sure.

He knew who was buried in that tomb with its dripping, sick-smelling candles and heaped wreaths. A rose that was not so sweet. The harlot.

He had been unable to do anything about this wickedness while the old King still lived, for they said he had loved her. The girl who lay in the tomb. Henry had sent many endowments to Godstow and asked that prayers be said for his lover's soul in perpetuity.

She would need them.

Love, the Bishop sneered, gazing down at the tomb as if he gazed upon the visage of Satan himself. There is no such thing as wholesome love save for that twixt brethren. Even marital love is tainted by the sin of Eve. And the King did not even marry the woman in the grave in the choir; she was just a creature bound to his lust and consumed by her own lusts. Just a concubine, one of many, for Henry II had been licentious indeed…

"This is a disgrace! Prioress Agnes!" He whirled on his heel and shouted at Godstow's prioress, who scuttled to his side, whey-faced, curtseying. "I cannot believe what I am seeing here! Why is veneration given to a…a whore?"

Mother Agnes's mouth opened but no sound would come out. She was new to her position as prioress of Godstow, and in complete awe of the mighty and holy Bishop of Lincoln. Eventually, she managed to stammer: "You…your Grace…I…"

"It's not hurting anyone!" A voice broke in, alone, defiant.

Bishop Hugh turned, scowling.

A plain little nun had broken free of the other nuns and stood beside the offending tomb.

"Who are you to contradict me?" thundered Hugh, glaring at the impertinent woman. "I will be the judge of what is right and wrong here. And this is wrong!"

"Is it?" The nun looked mutinous; not an appropriate look for a nun, who Hugh thought should be meek and mild. "I knew her. She was good and kind. The people come here to pray…for the sake of love. Not just carnal love, as you might think, Lord Bishop, but all love."

Bishop Hugh's face reddened, hearing her impertinent words. His wrath flared once more, causing him to shout, "People should not pray for love! They need to pray that their sins be taken away, that they keep their chastity and obedience! They certainly should not be asking favours of a vile, dead slattern."

Angrily he swung out with his jewel-encrusted crozier, striking off all the candles lined up atop the tomb chest. They crashed to the glazed tile floor, their wicks extinguished, smoke rising up in trails like ghostly fingers.

The nuns all jumped in fright at the desecration; Prioress Agnes swallowed and played nervously with her jet-beaded rosary.

Hugh continued his rampage, turning his attention onto the wreaths of roses adorning the tomb. Wildly he scattered them about the nave, sending their petals flying in a great hazy cloud; and then, in a final fit of pique, he stomped upon them, grinding them to shreds beneath his heels.

When he had completed his destruction, he balefully eyed the stripped-bared tomb once more, noticing for the first time that there was an inscription in Latin along the rim.

"*Adorent, Utque tibi detur requies Rosamunda precamu,*" Hugh murmured between gritted teeth. "Let them adore…and we pray that rest be given to you, Rosamund."

The Bishop fell silent for a moment, mouth working soundlessly as he digested what was written on the stonework. It was worse than he had imagined. Utter sacrilege.

With cruel mirth, he spat out mocking words, loud enough for all the onlookers to hear, "Here in this tomb lies the Rose of the World, not a pure rose. She who used to smell sweet still smells indeed —but now not so sweet."

Then he turned to confront Prioress Agnes, imperious, implacable. "Dismantle this tomb and take it from this House of God. Put it in the cemetery with the rest of the common folk. I charge you with seeing that my order is swiftly done, Prioress, and that sinners are not permitted to venerate its filthy occupant anymore."

"And…and if they do?" Prioress Agnes gulped, wringing her beads so hard that the string threatened to break.

"Then I shall inform the Pope of this disgrace…and see about excommunicating all those who partake of such unholiness!"

The next day, the tomb was dismantled, the bones removed from the lead lining and placed into a leather bag. A sweet smell emerged from the grave that made all the nuns marvel. Piece by piece, masons moved the tomb of Fair Rosamund from the choir to the wall of the sisters' Chapter House, where it remained for untold years…

Mist cloaked the turrets of my father's castle, hanging onto pinnacles and finials like ragged garments fit only for ghosts. With my two younger sisters, white-browed Amice and Lucie with her flowing mane of golden curls, I rode steadily on my bay palfrey toward Clifford Castle, following the long, winding path from the town of Hay, where our nurses had taken us to visit the market, a welcome distraction for three bored maidens long cooped indoors.

Winter had lashed the Marches with great severity that year. Snow blanketed the undulating rises of the land, rising to crests where an ill-wind licked it, while once-raging rivers had turned to ice, the cracked surfaces a deep and dangerous blue that beckoned the unwary toward a frigid, watery death.

With new storms arising ever day, blowing in from the distant Irish Sea, we girls had become as prisoners in the stronghold of Clifford Castle, locked behind the high stone walls, huddled before stoked braziers with our embroidery and our well-thumbed books, eager for spring and for the renewed life of a kinder season. We knew winter in the Marches could be cruel indeed, and already many babes and elders in the nearby village contracted perilous agues—and the graveyards grew full of pathetic earthen mounds frosted with snow.

Even in the castle, far warmer than any peasants' hut, with its burning central fires and furs on the bed, we knew fear. Illness stalked the unwary, even behind stout walls. The chaplain said prayers daily to ward harm away from us all—but particularly away from my brother Walter, little Watkin, my father's heir, who was only three, and for the latest babe, also a boy, named Richard for his grandsire. It must have worked, for Watkin and Richard survived without a solitary sniffle, and now the sun was coming back and the snow melting.

I stared up at the fortress from the back of my steed, at stonework dim and age-worn amidst the floating vapours of the mists. Standing on its green mound, Clifford Castle was stern of aspect and rather old fashioned, its walls patched with different coloured blocks after a hundred frays with the Welsh, yet I could not imagine living anywhere else, not even in nearly Hereford town or fabled, near-mythical London. Built nigh on a hundred years ago by William FitzOsbern, first Earl of Herefordshire, the castle seemed to me a place of dreams, even when residing in harsh winter's grip. As did the surrounding village, with its cottages huddled at the solid foot of St Mary's church, their crude pottery chimneys smoking into the cold night.

Llanfair, some of the villagers called the church instead of the more prosaic St Mary's. I let the name slide off my tongue, trying to emulate the pronunciation of the locals. An outlandish but beautiful name. Church of Mary, the Virgin. Mary…Fair…

This whole region of the Wye reeked of age, of ancient myth; the odd tongue of the Welsh existed even on the English side of the border, although in ever decreasing amounts, and gave itself well to tales of ghosts and heroes and the Bendith y Mamau, the Mother's Blessings. Every lake had a lady who swam beneath the obscured surface, every river a hungry water-goddess who ate small children, every hummock a sleeping king clad in pale grave-gold, waiting to rise and ride when summoned by the needy.

My reverie was broken as Lucie rode up beside me on her pony and clutched my sleeve in a gloved hand. Youngest of the Clifford sisters, Lucie was named for Light, and the name suited her well, for she was ever a bright spark in both temperament and looks—her curls a radiant golden halo, her wide, teasing eyes the colour of the deepening sky after sunset.

"Rosamund!" she cried. "Did you see her? The Green Lady! I saw you looking up at the castle, an expression of wonder on your face! Did you see her?"

The Green Lady! I started and then smiled. Oh yes, she was Clifford Castle's own spirit, to go with the lake maids and river-hags and sleeping kings that dwelt in the surrounding landscape. One of our old nurses, Olwyn, had told us her sad tale, a tale of betrayal and blood. Centuries ago, long before the castle was built, a beautiful girl who lived in the valley had fallen in love with a young lord who came out of the south to claim the land. Her beauty had captivated him, and she had surrendered her maidenhood to him willingly, but once he had taken his pleasure, he proved a false lover. Scorning to wed a humble but beautiful girl, he sought instead the hand of a foreign princess, and heeding the advice of a wicked enchanter, decided to slay his trusting leman. The necromancer had told him that the blood and body of an innocent placed below a wall would make it stand forever—and that is what he wanted most, a sturdy fortress where he might grow a new dynasty with his princess from afar.

So, the maid who loved him became not his bride, but bride of the dark earth below, wedded to the dark soil, the earthworm, the mould of the grave. And the castle grew up over her bones, a modest structure at first with a single curtain wall and dank, dark donjon, then growing taller and more imposing, with bartizans and crenels and machicolations. The young lord built a castle to last on the ruins of his lover's life but his line did not last. He died, his heirs died, and others held their keep in their stead...but the Green Lady was not gone, for all that her cruel tormentor burned in Hell. Wreathed in ivy, she would tap on the window shutters with her long, curved nails, seeking her lost life, the lost lover who had betrayed her. Gossips claimed her appearance betokened a broken heart, a disaster, a change, even death...

Mother had been most put out when Lucie, Amice and I were caught chattering about the Green Lady. Most sternly, she told us that this legend was naught but foolish nonsense, and that the tapping we heard on the shutters at night was merely the ivy fronds grown too long. The eastern tower, where we children slept in the nursery, was furled in growth, and father would soon have to employ someone to hew it down before it ruined the castle's stonework.

Olwyn was dismissed by mother for filling our heads with 'unseemly pagan tales' and despite our pleas to let her stay, she was sent grumbling down to the village—along with a pack of other castle servants who bore Welsh names or Welsh tongues...for trouble was brewing in the Marches and no Welshman could be trusted. My father could be a hard man and would take no chances with the loyalties of his household. He was sworn to the cause of King Henry and knew that soon Henry would make another incursion into Wales in an attempt to curb the fractious princes who dwelt in castles high as eagle's eyries, with bards filling their wild heads full of the glorious deeds of long-dead ancestors.

Bouncing in her saddle, Lucie was still babbling about the Green Lady and waving her arm about like some kind of mooncalf. She was still at an age when legends were, without question, true.

Amice rolled her dark eyes and glanced at me expectantly from beneath the frilled rim of her headdress. We often endured Lucie's rambunctious chatter, but mother did not countenance talk of supernatural beings and the nurses were all in earshot, for all that they looked like placid, harmless great cows as they sat slouched on the backs of their tame nags.

"Enough, Lucie," I said at length, driving my palfrey close to my little sister so the nurses could not overhear. "I saw nothing. I was just…daydreaming…"

"*I* saw something," said Lucie steadfastly, her chin taking on a defiant tilt. "I think you did too."

"I did not. And you were surely just imagining that you did. The Green Lady is merely an ancient story further embroidered by Olwyn, to frighten and to entertain those who enjoy that sort of thing! It is not true. You should be growing out of such fancies now; after all, father has arranged your marriage to Hugh de Say of Stokesay. You should be thinking of that future, of how to be the wife Hugh expects. He won't want someone blithering about ghosts like a loon."

Lucie's face fell and then became mutinous. In unladylike fashion, she thrust out her tongue. "It will be years before I marry Hugh; I am nowhere near the age that we might cohabit. If someone should be making herself ideal for a husband, it should be you, Rosamund. I wonder…Why has father not found a match for you, when you are the oldest of us three maidens? Maybe no one likes you and he cannot…"

"Lucie, what an unkind thing to say!" Amice frowned from the back of her placid mare. "Rosamund will have a husband, I am sure. Father has not found the right one for her yet, that is all."

"But he has found one for you, Amice, hasn't he? Osbern FitzHugh of Richard's Castle. We are both matched to good, powerful men, despite being the younger daughters of our House. Why not Rosamund?"

"Is there ever any sense or design in what father does?" Amice let out an exasperated sigh. She was but one year younger than I, but seemed older in her mannerisms, a practical no-nonsense girl tall for her age and whose looks would be termed handsome, rather than beautiful, except for her skin; it was like pure cream and her hands as fair as those of Iseult of the White Hands in the old tale of Tristan. "You know the wheels in father's mind are always turning. He will have a most grand future planned out for Rosamund, I am certain. Unless…he wants her to become a nun."

Head on one side, she glanced thoughtfully at me and then at little Lucie, her veil floating out on the breeze like the mist wreathing the hills, the houses, the battlements. "I doubt he'd let a first-born daughter go to be a nun, though. Maybe there has been a mistake.

Rosamund will marry Hugh de Say, and you will be sent to join a nunnery, Lucie!"

Lucie gave an angry and vaguely fearful squeal and pounded her boots against the side of her steed—a tame, barrel-shaped pony brought down from the Welsh mountains. She was not mature enough to ride fully grown horses like Amice and I. "You are making fun of me now!" she said, pulling ahead of me and almost crashing her mount into the sullen, muddy-footed guards that surrounded our little entourage, keeping us safe from any assaults by brigands on the road to Hay. "I hate you…both of you!"

"What have I done?" I raised my brows. "Merely told you to speak not of spooks and sprites lest we be chided for it! You spoke nastily to me, not the reverse. Poor Hugh de Say, if he should have such a shrew to wife."

Lucie's shoulders shuddered and she now began to weep, showing herself for the little girl that she truly was. Her nurse Havis, riding near her golden-haired charge, began to make clucking noises like some oversized hen as she made to soothe her. "All I asked about was the Green Lady. I saw her, I did. Something is going to happen, Rosamund. To one of us…or all of us. Father is going to be fighting the Welsh. The King will be on the move. And the Green Lady…she has betokened whatever is to come."

I was silent as my small sister, still snuffling, pushed on toward the gatehouse with its spiked portcullis, and Amice glanced over and shrugged her slender shoulders in dismay. A knot of nervous fear coiled within me, though, despite showing disdain toward Lucie's supposed vision. For, although I had not admitted it, seconds before she grasped my sleeve, I too had seen a figure high on the tower near the jutting rim of the parapet. A sinuous figure coiled in green that swiftly vanished into the ivy cocoon below.

The Green Lady, harbinger of change—and sometimes of doom.

We gathered in the Great Hall, the entire Clifford family, circled by our retainers and servants. Mother, Margaret de Tosney, had left her quarters to join us; she looked careworn, older than her age, her face drained of colour till she almost seemed an alabaster effigy. She pressed one hand to her back, supporting herself; beneath her green brocade robes, her belly was swollen with yet another pregnancy—her sixth in all and her second within two years. Our baby brother Richard was at her side, held fast in the arms of a fat wet-nurse. And so too was little Watkin, the heir to Clifford, already looking very martial despite being but three summers old, wearing our father's device on his tunic and with a child's wooden sword bound to his belt. Watkin was ignoring his older sisters; even at his young age, he had acquired the notion that girls were somehow beneath his contempt. It was not surprising, really; he was the apple of father's eye while we were merely wealth to be traded away.

"I hope father marries him off to some shrew," said Lucie balefully, eyes hooded and rosebud lips curling in an unmannerly way. After I had called her a shrew for unfairly berating me outside the castle, it had become her favourite word for any female she didn't like, from the nurses to the old cheesemonger in the village who would not let her have more than one sample, and even to mother who, tired out, chided her when she became too rambunctious.

Overhearing her speak so rudely about our parent, I had dragged her into a corner behind the Arras tapestry and slapped her on the cheek. With mother clearly unwell due to the coming child, I had assumed her role as disciplinarian; better me, I thought, than father, who could be unduly harsh in punishments.

"What madness has got into you, Lucie? Never speak so of our mother!" I warned, my fingers biting into her shoulders. "Never forget who she is! A de Tosney, descended from the esteemed Lord Raoul, who fought beside the Conqueror at Hastings. She also comes from the line of Waltheof, Earl of Huntingdon, a great Saxon noble; his daughter Adelise was our grandmother. She is kin by marriage to Scotland's King. So do not speak of her as if she were of common stock. A shrew, indeed. For shame!"

Lucie had sulked, pouted, pulled away and flounced off. But I wagered she would never dare call mother names again, even in anger.

My gaze drifted uneasily about the packed Great Hall, wondering what was to come. Father had ordered us all to gather, and no one dared gainsay him, even though unwell or busy with their trades. He demanded to be obeyed in all things, perhaps because, in his youth, none had listened to him, for then he was no one.

Highborn as our lady-mother was, we could not say the same for our sire, Walter Clifford. He was, to some degree, a self-made man. Once, long before our births, he had merely been steward of Clifford castle, and had succeeded to his high offices at Clifford only through marrying our mother, a de Tosney—how such an improbable event had occurred was never discussed, but I had heard unpleasant whispers down in the village, where tongues sometimes ran freer than they ought. Stories that claimed father had ravished mother the very night the old de Tosney lord died and forced her to become his bride through shame. I had covered my ears, refusing to listen. Father could be hard, braying, selfish, officious and cruel…but surely not a defiler of women. As far as any of us knew, he had no mistresses, no bastards; if anything, his position as a grand lord in the Marches was his one true love.

Besides Clifford castle, a number of other manors had been granted him for good service to the King, and several more inherited from his childless uncles, Drogo and Walter. His father, Richard FitzPontz, had died young and left him nothing, which always irked him even years after the event, as if his father had died merely to spite him. He was so troubled by the penury FitzPontz had left him in, he even cast off his proper patronymic, FitzRichard, and was known solely as Clifford, after our castle. And so was I known, too—Rosamund Clifford, the Rose of the World.

A clarion blared, its shrill note bouncing off the sweating walls with their dangling, soot-smeared tapestries and carven heads of kings and saints. Cloak swinging, father swept into the Hall and strode purposefully towards the fire-pit where we had gathered. A well-built man of middling height, with muscle not yet turned to fat, he had auburn hair cut short at the back and straight across the forehead, and small, suspicious, green-flecked eyes. No one could call him handsome, pugnacious rather, with a short, blunt nose and a thrusting square jaw; fortunately, we girls took after our maternal side in feature. I, alone, inherited something of my father's heritage—while Lucie was blonde and Amice brown-haired, I had inherited Walter Clifford's rich russet hair.

He nodded his head towards mother, Lady Margaret, and took her hand, guiding her towards the dais at the far end of the Hall, where he saw her seated and then sat down beside her. Watkin trundled over to stand dutifully at his knee; the image of his sire, even down to the same defiant expression, so odd on a little boy of his tender age.

"What is this all about, Walter?" I heard mother say, her voice tired. "I am very weary. The child weighs heavy on me."

"You shall see!" Father's lips quirked; he seldom gave a true smile—he was not a man for levity, and besides, he had broken several teeth in a brawl. "I believe you shall enjoy this, Margaret. You and our daughters."

His gaze flicked to his girls, standing stiff and starched in our best gowns—he hated any sign of slovenliness, even in the winter when it was hard to wash linens or remove the lice from one's garb. "Not my sort of thing, truth be told…but I have minstrels coming into Clifford. Minstrels and musicians."

"Minstrels!" Lucie's voice sounded, surprised; then she clapped her hand to her mouth, fearing chastisement for her outburst.

"Minstrels, indeed!" Mother's dark brows rose; she looked near as shocked as Lucie. "We have not had that sort of entertainment here…for years."

"No, I deem such singing frivolous—and what is better than sung hymns or plain chant? Certainly not warbling and carolling," said father, with a dismissive snort. "But there will be minstrels here today. And you, Margaret, shall choose the best from amongst them."

"What is the occasion?" A slight frown line deepened on mother's forehead. "This levity is most unlike you, Walter."

Father's lips widened in a grin. "I have received news, excellent news. You are aware that the Welsh have grown restive again and that the King is filled with great displeasure by their raids and fractiousness. Well, he is to move against them, at last…and he will be coming to Castle Clifford! I would not have him think we are rustic simpletons without the niceties current at his court; and for all that he is a mighty warrior, I have heard he likes music. And dancing."

Mother's face whitened, as a flurry of whispers ran through the assembly in the Hall. "His Grace, King Henry, coming here?"

"You heard me, wife. He will come. It will be a great honour, and…" his eyes glittered "with any luck, a great opportunity to rise in his favour."

Mother leant back in her chair as if overcome, while her ladies fluttered around her, cosseting and fussing, bringing wine for her to sip. Baby Richard began to wail, sensing his dam's distress, and his clucking wet-nurse bore him back to the nursery, just as the minstrels and musicians began to arrive—a motley crew who stepped nervously into the Great Hall, clutching their shawms, psalteries, and sackbuts.

Amice, Lucie and I craned to see. Minstrels and troubadours were almost like magical beings, full of tales from far off lands and singing songs of sad, lost love. We had all heard gossip (although most likely false) of handsome young singers strumming harps and winning the favours of ladies much above their station. Ladies they ran away with before being hunted down and killed by jealous, wicked lords who had no inkling about true love....

"D'you think any of them are handsome?" Amice whispered into my ear.

I gazed at the gaggle of men—a toothless greybeard in a red felt cap, a skinny youth with lank blond hair, a short, red-faced man with a gap in his teeth and pox scars all over him.

"No!" I responded, shaking my head emphatically, as she eyed the newcomers "Definitely not! Let us hope their singing is more attractive than their looks!"

Amice stifled a giggle with her sleeve. "By St Uncumber's beard, I'd rather join a convent than become entangled with any one of them! I am more interested in the King coming here! Do you think we will be introduced to him? What do you suppose he's like, Rosamund?"

I shrugged. "I have heard that he is fearsome in battle, wild as a boar; and that his temper when roused is terrible. That he chases women and foams on the rushes if he is denied the one he wants."

"But is he handsome?" asked Amice.

"They say so," I replied. "It is said his father Geoffrey Plantagenet was handsome too."

"Geoffrey of the Sprig of Broom," said Amice. "Do you think the King's hair might be golden as the broom for which he's named?"

I shook my head. "I heard it is reddish...to match his fiery temper."

Lucie, butting in, tittered slyly. "You and the King might be well matched then, Rosamund. Red-tressed and evil-tempered. Maybe he will desire you, as you are both so alike!"

"Lucie, your tongue is too free!" Hot colour rioted in my cheeks.

Amice jumped to my defence. "For Jesu's sake, Lucie, don't say such things when King Henry arrives. It might prove embarrassing. I think mother should keep you in the nursery with the babes; you don't know what is appropriate and what is not. For all his reputation, the King is hardly going to run after our Rosamund, not right under father's nose!"

As Amice spoke, a cold shudder went through me, instantly banishing the heat that had flooded my face. I was puzzled and confused; why did such fear grip my heart? Old Olwyn would have claimed a hare was bounding over my unknown future grave; she was full of such lore, dark and not terribly Christian.

But I was Christian, and I was a good maiden, dutiful to God and to my parents. To my King too, of course...in a chaste, subservient way. And yet...while the household around me buzzed with excitement at the thoughts of playing host to a King, I shivered and my stomach lurched. Henry, son of the fierce old Empress who had waged war with her usurping cousin Stephen, almost bringing England to its knees in a bloody battle for the Crown... Henry Plantagenet hovered ominously in my thoughts like a black-winged raven, and I did not understand why.

Chapter Three—In a Forest Darkly.

Preparations for the King's visit gripped the household. Old rushes and mats were peeled from the flagstones and servants toiled with tubs of water to scrub the floors clean. Others brought fresh mats, newly woven from river-reeds by the villagers and laid them down. Father, poring over his account books like some possessed demon, even imported several rugs—great, furry things with heraldic designs stitched into them. He would not let us touch them, but guarded them jealously—they were only for royal feet to tread on. Moth-eaten and smoke blackened tapestries were torn down and new ones hung up to replace them, and the potboys were ordered to polish the plate until they could see their faces in it.

Mother smiled wearily, watching this hive of activity overwhelm her home. Father had the garderobes sluiced out and packed with herbs, and he finally agreed to the maintenance she wanted—removing the ivy that clung to the exterior of the nursery tower. Green fronds drifted through the air as intrepid servants clambered over the stonework, binding themselves to the crenels with sturdy ropes as they hacked at the vines with great, curved sickles.

As I watched the ribbons of ivy flutter down to the courtyard, I wondered if the Green Woman would be angry at such desecration …and then chided myself for still paying heed to such a childish tale, especially as I had castigated Lucie for it. But as the easterly wind blew in, spattering me with cut leaves that smelt of sap, I shivered and slammed the shutters.

Father's attention to the preparations for King Henry's arrival soon extended beyond new tapestries and other comforts and touched on his three daughters. New gowns were brought to us, of imported silk, taffeta and brocade. Father seemed, in particular, to have taken new interest in us; odd, as he had always referred to us as the 'pack of interminable whingeing girls' in the days before Walter and Richard were born.

Sitting in his high seat, carved out of bog oak with huge armrests fashioned into roaring lion's heads, he examined me with a critical eye as I showed off my new gown—grass green silk with paler cendal lining, setting off my fiery colouring. "Turn around, child," he ordered. "Let me see that it hangs well on you, after I have paid such good money for it."

I twirled as daintily as I could but, uncomfortable under his scrutiny, I stumbled and trod on my long hem. Rather unexpectedly, my father's eyes blazed with anger and he clutched the arms of his chair till his knuckles whitened. "Christ Almighty…" he voice was harsh with anger, "I have paid governesses aplenty to teach you womanly arts, and yet still you bumble around like an ungainly ox! You will shame me before the King with such a buffoonish performance!"

Out of the corner of my eye, I spotted Lucie and Amice hovering in the background, and embarrassment flooded over me; I wanted to weep. Lucie was laughing, her sleeve pressed to her mouth to muffle the noise.

"Father," I said boldly, my head tilted up in an arrogant fashion, "I am sure the King is coming to Clifford Castle to speak of war, not to comment on the grace or lack thereof, in the daughter of a minor border lord."

Lucie and Amice's faces froze, their smirks and titters vanishing instantly. Father's face also froze, becoming a block of ice. Before I could even move, his huge hand, speckled with dark hairs like a boar's bristles, shot up and struck the side of my head, sending me sprawling in a heap before his feet.

Lucie uttered a small shriek, Amice elbowed her into silence, lest father's wrath turn on them too.

Leaning over, father grasped my arm and wrenched me roughly to my feet. "You will never speak so to me again, do you hear, girl? And you will dance for me, and for the King, whenever I ask of it. And I will make certain you do not look like a lumbering ox in front of his Grace. Now dance!"

I leapt away from him, and a musician, one of the two hired to play for the King, began to nervously play a jaunty air on a flute.

"Dance!" My father yelled again, his cheeks mottled red. A droplet of spit quivered on his lip.

I danced.

"Dance!" he cried once more, as my feet flagged, uncertain of the steps, the heavy unfamiliar gown dragging at my ankles. "Goddamn you, you clumsy baggage! Pick up your feet!"

And as I tried yet again, my face rigid with fear, sweat springing on my body, "Dance, goddamn you, with a smile on your face and some lightness in your step. You look like you are attending a funeral. Smile and toss back your hair…yes, unbraid your hair, Rosamund. I want to see your bloody hair!"

I began to wonder if father was drunk, so strange was his behaviour. With shaking hands, I dragged off the bindings on my hair and shook it free. Dark red fire, it tumbled over my shoulders and down to my waist. Waves and curls, my bane, twisted around me, a burning cloud—though, I imagined, not so red in hue as my flaming cheeks.

"Better!" father mumbled, stroking his beard. "Better. Now dance…again. With some life… The King is coming soon. Within days!"

I could take no more of his goading. "You would think he is coming to marry me, the way you are behaving!" I cried, all caution thrown to the wind, then as I saw his huge hand raised for another ear-ringing blow, I fled the hall and ran for safety with the speed of a fleeing deer. His shouts, wordless, threatening, chased after me.

Heart hammering, breath harsh in my lungs, I scurried into the bailey. Outside, it was raining; cold droplets struck my face, mingling with my tears. What was my father playing at? I felt frightened, as if I stood on top of a vast precipice, gazing down at…what?

A rumble of thunder came from the sullen clouds, hanging like a pendulous swollen belly over the castle's towers. Near at hand, a serving girl shrieked, affrighted by the sound; I saw porters, sewers, and stableboys run for cover.

I should have run for cover too, but sudden madness possessed me. I sprang for the gate—wide open, its brass fittings gleaming in the stormlight—it was still long before curfew. One of the guards on duty, a spotty-faced youngster scarcely older than I, saw me and cried out a jittery warning but the gusts of wind whipped his words away.

Lifting my skirts like an unseemly hoyden, I dashed past the guard and stumbled down the rock-strewn slope of the castle motte, the torrential rain forming a little river that washed past me, laving my ankles in mud and pebbles. I wondered offhandedly if the river below the walls would flood; when it did, a marsh grew around the base of Clifford castle, making the fortress an island cut off from the village. I hoped it would and that my father would stay within and that the King of England would never come there—the excitement the Clifford daughters had first felt when hearing of his planned visit, had turned into unhappy turmoil for me.

I decided not to head for the village; too much chance of being spotted and tongues would wag and news go straight up to the castle. Instead, I hurried towards the copse of dark green trees on the rise beyond the sodden cluster of cottages. Capped by cloud, boughs heavy with water, they formed a shadowed cavern that would provide a near-perfect shelter where I could avoid my father for a while. My unexpected and unauthorised absence would be near enough to a punishment for him—he would be terrified that some Welsh riever would ride by and carry me off, ruining any plans he had for my future.

I entered the stern line of trees, which marched along the top of the rise like straight-backed soldiers. Oaks clung to rock; a carpet of drenched moss muffled the sound of my footfalls. A holly tree swayed in the rising wind, showering blood-hued berries. Dragging my damp and now-ruined dress (I scowled, knowing I would get a thrashing for that!) I climbed up to the top of a mighty boulder, furred by the moss and by little clinging shrubs.

Sitting down, I hugged my knees. Rain leaked through gaps in the boughs above, turning my loose hair the colour of dark wine. Gradually my anger at father began to fade. Abject misery set in. I started to sniffle. I wanted to get warm. Night was coming in fast now; the days were still short, and the light beyond the trees had paled to a sombre blue colour. To be out after dark in these troubled, debatable lands was not wise…

Shivering, I stretched out my cold legs, wriggling my feet to restore my circulation. The wind whispered, snickering in the branches overhead. Carefully I began to slide off the rock, seeking the safety of the trail back to the village, which was already obscured by a hazy twilit gloom.

And then I heard an ominous sound. Pausing, I listened again, straining my ears. My blood froze in my veins. There it was again. The dull thud of a horse's hoofs, half muffled by mouldering leaf fall, from deeper within the grove, up where the land swept to meet an even higher wooded ridge.

I had to get away! I could take no chances as to whether this mounted newcomer was friend or foe! Fear bubbled up in my heart; why had I been so foolish, so wilful?

I began to run, darting like a deer between the boles of the trees.

Suddenly an arrow slammed into the ground near me, ripping up the mulch and embedding itself deep into the earth. A terrified scream ripped unbidden from my lips as I spun round.

"By Christ's Beard—a girl!" I heard a male voice cry out. Heavily accented, the stranger spoke the best court Norman French…even as he swore his disrespectful oath about Our Lord.

The trees swayed, tore apart. A man on a strong bay horse burst through. He stared at me, eyes blazing, and like a frightened rabbit I stood still, too afraid to move, staring straight back.

Even though he was mounted, I could see by the length of his legs that the rider was not a tall man but one who was short and stocky, heavy with muscle. Deep reddish-brown hair was clipped across the brow, much like my father's in style but thicker, curlier in texture. His face was full of fury, but if not so angry would have been a pleasant enough face, with a strong chin and long straight nose. He wore clothes of midnight-black—a wealthy man's garment, for black dye was expensive.

"What did you think you were doing, girl?" he barked. "I could have killed you!"

I was too afraid to move, to shout back that these were my father's lands, and what was he doing here? My gaze slipped to the bow in his hands; well, yes, I could see what he was doing. He was hunting, and he had no right to do so!

He began driving his big bay steed towards me. He looked down at me, disdainful. I could see his eyes now, under thick dark brows; indeterminate colour, mixed grey, green and amber. Almost wolfish in their intensity. "Cat got your tongue, girl? Pah!" He spoke to himself, his mouth quirking cruelly, "She cannot understand me, the slattern probably speaks only the Saxon tongue…or Welsh."

In a swift movement, he swung down from his steed, letting the reigns drag.

I still stood there like a mooncalf, affrighted by my brush with death. As he approached, the stranger was looking at me differently now, his wrath evaporating. He gazed at me in a way no man had gazed at me before. A thrill I did not understand rushed through me.

"You're a pretty thing," he murmured, in truth talking to himself rather than to me, since he thought I could not understand him. "Who are you to be wandering out here unchaperoned?" He grinned. "Well, that could go the better for me…"

His arm shot out with the speed of a striking snake, caught me unaware, and dragged me towards him. I tried to cry out in protest but his mouth descended on mine, cutting off my scream as he forced my lips apart with brutal lust. I beat at him with my fists, furious…and terrified.

"How dare you!" I managed to wrench my head away and shout out in Norman French, trying vainly to sound authoritative rather than shrill. "Unhand me. I am not some village wench for you to tumble at will. I am Rosamund de Clifford, Lord Walter's daughter! My father will hunt you down…and…and kill you. Kill you!"

The man's hands fell from me and he looked startled. Then he began to laugh. Somehow, his mirth made me feel even more afraid. But he did not make to touch me again. "Lord Clifford's daughter! Dare I ask what you were doing running about the forest at near dark?"

"You may *not* ask!" I shot back, fear making my tongue sharp. I could not afford to let such a bold one know of my true terror in his presence. I had felt the strength in him…and the desire…In a moment, he could have me on my back and proceed to ravish me and I would have no recourse. "I ask, who are you, who dare to hunt on my father's lands? You have no right. It is forbidden."

He took a deep breath. "Do you not know? I hunt where I will, as is my right. I am Curtmantle."

"I know neither your name nor who you are, nor do I want to!" I returned, shaking my head. "Only that you shouldn't be here in this forest, nor should you have laid hands upon me!"

He began to laugh again, a rich, deep sound, rolling like thunder. For some reason, the sound thrilled me as well as heightened my fear. "You truly do not know! Ah, sweet little Rosamund, Rose of the World, let me tell you….'

A horn suddenly sounded off in the darkling wood behind him, its echoes falling dead amidst the storm-tossed trees. "Ah, the hunting party comes…" my assailant muttered, glancing over one muscled shoulder.

I saw my chance, took it. Whirling on my heels, my bedraggled gown clutched in knotted hands, I ran as fast as my legs would carry me away from this strange, unsettling man.

"Wha..?" I heard him shout, as he realised I had made a dash for freedom.

Thank Jesu and the saints, he did not pursue but let me flee, stumbling out of the woods and down toward the village and castle. Mayhap he thought he dared not race his horse on the rain-slicked, unfamiliar ground; maybe he had realised how unwise it was to insult or defoul the daughter of a notable Marcher lord.

Truth be told, though, I did not think it was the latter, as much as it would have pleased me to think I had shamed him with my stern words. As I ran, my hair flying, my dress slopping water and mud dappling my shamefully bare legs, I heard in the distance the strange man laughing...*Laughing*...

"You said what!" My father's hand, always over eager to smite, struck against my cheek. For the second time in as many days, I hit the hard flagstones of the castle's Great Hall, to the gasps and cries of the servants, who then averted their gazes and scurried about like beetles emerging from a broken piece of wood.

"Walter!" Whey-faced, holding her distended belly, mother eased herself from her chair of estate. "Please, do not…"

Father pinned her with a ferocious stare. "Go, Margaret—retire and take care of my newest son within your belly. Do not raise my anger further. You know what she has done…"

I struggled to my feet, mud-caked, shivering, furious and fearful all at once. "Well, if I have done some wrong, tell me! I thought you would have a care that strangers are abroad on your lands, hunting the game…and…and molesting your daughter."

He glowered at me, nostrils flaring open and shut like those of an enraged bull. "Little, stupid, ill-educated fool. Curtmantle! Are you so locked in your female frivolities, that you do not know who Curtmantle is?"

I shook my head slowly; raindrops spattered on the floor. The name meant nothing to me. Nothing at all. Short-cloak.

"What do I pay your tutors for?" father began, teeth gritted. "To fill your muddled head with capricious nothings…"

"To teach me to sing and embroider…and dance…all the things a girl should know. You were certainly determined to see me practice dancing skills earlier on and cared not if I knew the difference between a cow and a capon!"

Once again, my loose tongue got hold of me; my nurse said my disrespectful ways were on account of my red hair, an unlucky trait if ever there was one. Men might say they admired my locks but few forgot that the traitor Judas's hair was red, and that harlots often dyed their hair such a hue to get attention.

I cowered, expecting another blow. Mother's brow creased; she looked a little faint and fanned herself with her hand. Amice, who had crept into the hall, steadied her elbow.

Father did not strike me. Instead, he pressed his glaring, puce face to mine. "Dear daughter…" His voice was as sharp as a blade. "Curtmantle is Henry. Henry…Henry, King of England, Lord of

Normandy, Anjou and Aquitaine…and you, a foolish, wilful chit, have insulted him!"

My head spun. "The King!"

"Aye, the King!" Father's lips were now near my ear, moving fast as he spoke harsh words. "He has arrived earlier than expected, that much is clear. He will be looking for feasting, drink…and comforts. The King, Rosamund, is a lusty man of many appetites, much in the manner of his grandfather, Henry I…"

Not quite understanding, I blinked at him. The King was known for his love of women, and his grandfather, sire of his mother the Empress Maud, had an almost unnumbered pack of bastards. But what had any of that to do with me?

Sudden knowledge dawned in my brain, and I felt a flush rise to the roots of my hair. "You…you…I cannot believe what I hear, father. You…you would play the part of a procurer! With your own daughter!"

"Be silent! Do you want all these gawping oafs to hear?" Father grasped my arm and hustled me into an alcove away from the prying eyes of the servants and from my worried mother and sister. Behind a rich drapery, he roughly thrust me onto a stone window seat. "Now you will listen to me, Rosamund. You are my daughter to give or withhold, as I will. As my eldest, I always had great plans for you, for you have a rare beauty even if you do not yet realise it."

"Great plans?" I began to cry now, despite willing myself to hold back the tears. "You plan to give me to the King like the gift of a hawk or a hound. He will have his pleasure and discard me. My life shall be ruined. What, by Christ, can be gained by that?"

"Favour for me!" spat father. "And if you play your part right, perhaps a life you have never even dreamed of!"

"As a mistress? A concubine?" I said scornfully, wiping at my damp eyes.

"You may rise further that that, Rosamund." A grim smile twisted his lips. "And I would rise in your wake, to new wealth and prominence. I long to leave these Borderlands and deal with civilised men!"

"How would I rise?" I said scornfully. "Do you think he'd make me Queen? King Henry is married to Eleanor of Aquitaine, one of the great beauties of our time. The minstrels sing lewd songs about wishing to bed her! *If the world were all mine, from the sea to the Rhine, I would give up its charms, if the fair Queen of England lay in my arms.* That's what they sing!"

"They sing such songs because Eleanor is known to be immoral," said father. "Why, 'tis said she lay with the King's father, Geoffrey Plantagenet, and with her own uncle and maybe even that paynim, Saladin! She has produced heirs for Henry; but he will tire of her, if he hasn't already. I've heard tell they fight like cat and dog. You will be far more suitable than this woman, who is so much older than her husband too. Your blood is good, you have no blemish on your character, and you are not of foreign stock."

"I think you are mad," I said, shaking my head. "I am a young maiden. I would sooner seek a convent that be some…light o' love to any man, even a King! Have you not thought of the consequences, should your plots go awry? He might go forth from here and never summon me again, leaving me with child…" I shuddered, convulsed with sickness. Like most maids, I dreamed of an honourable marriage, my own manor, legitimate children who would inherit…not some clandestine affair. Even with the greatest man in the land.

 Father waved his hand dismissively. "A bastard would not be a problem. Being the King's mistress would be an approving seal upon you. It would be no hardship to find you a suitable husband, and who knows, the King might even acknowledge the child and give you a pension for life."

I thought of the rumours about my parents' own marriage, about power-hungry Walter FitzRichard forcing bereaved Margaret de Tosney into wedlock in his quest for lands and power. I now firmly believed the whispers must be true. No wonder mother always looked cowed. How, I hated him in that instant.

"But you might have ruined all by your behaviour today," father grumbled, ignoring the hateful glare I sent in his direction. "Running like a mad hare from King Henry and speaking to his Grace in a discourteous manner. Still, there is no helping it now. What will be, will be. Maybe he will have forgotten by the time he arrives at Clifford Castle. You had best hope so, girl." He grasped my shoulders; his fingertips bit through soggy cloth into the tender flesh of my shoulders. "You will be biddable to Henry, girl. You will do whatever he asks of you."

"Let me go," I managed to croak, and then pushed him aside and rushed toward my chambers. Reaching them, I threw myself face down on my bed, avoiding Lucie's wild questions about my meeting with the King. Her voice went on and on, shrill and excited, "What was he like?

Was he handsome? Was he tall? Short? Fat? Did he try to kiss you? I heard he is a lecher. What is a 'lecher', Rosamund?"

I could not answer her. I just hid my face in the coverlet and cried.

"It is not fair!" Amice's voice rose in an unhappy wail. The calmest in temperament of the three daughters of Walter Clifford, it was rare to hear her cry out in anger or dismay.

Today was different, though. King Henry had arrived, his soldiers in their jingling mail filling the castle bailey, and word had come from father, passed down like God's judgment—Amice was to give me her new gown since I had ruined mine in my escapade in the forest. The laundresses, despite their best efforts, could not remove all the mud stains, and threads were pulled loose and fabric damaged.

Mother, who had risen from her bed to oversee us being dressed by our attendants, sighed and shook her head. "Be silent, Amice. You have a decent enough gown to wear…the white diasper one with the pearls at the neck."

"But it's old!" Amice's lip quivered as if she would cry. "I will look like a frumpy matron before the King, the plainest of Walter Clifford's daughters."

Lucie was having her golden curls brushed, as her ladies held a small bronze mirror before her round, glowing young face. "That you might look dowdy to the King doesn't matter to father," she said, rather astutely for a maiden of such tender years. "It is clear he wants King Henry to gaze favourably upon Rosamund rather than either of us!"

"Rosamund probably won't even fit the gown!" cried Amice with a rare outburst of petulance. "She's much fatter than me! You'll have to get a seamstress to let out the bodice—she has udders big as a cow's!"

"Amice, be silent!" Mother cried in exasperation, as Lucie choked back a high-pitched laugh. She gestured to one of the ladies in waiting. "Tilda, take Lady Amice from the room and sit with her until she comes to her senses and begins to act like a civilised young woman and not an uncouth village hussy. Lucie, your chattering and laughter is no help to me either… Go with your sister and wait until you are summoned."

Amice and Lucie left the chamber with their attendant ladies gathered around them. I was left alone with mother. I took her hands in mine, hoping against hope she would offer me some words of comfort, some sign she would help me.

"I don't want to go into the Hall tonight," I said.

"You must. It is your father's will."

"I am afraid."

"You must conquer your fear."

"Mother…" My mouth was dry. "You must know why father wants the King to take note of me."

No reply. She did know.

"I do not want this, I beg you…"

"What you want is immaterial, Rosamund," she snapped back.

"Do you want this?"

Silence again.

"There, I knew it…you do not approve. Speak for me, mother…Father might listen to you."

A harsh little laugh emerged from the corner of her mouth. Her face looked pinched and old, full of remembered bitterness. "He won't listen to me. When has he ever? He would never take no for an answer…If he had, we would never have been wed." Abruptly she clutched her pregnant belly, as if in pain.

"Mother!" I cried, afraid. I reached to steady her.

"I am fine, I am fine!" she cried, pushing me away. "But do not be difficult. It will bring pain to me…and to you. Just do as your father says and as King Henry says, it will be easier that way. Do not fight your destiny. You are old enough to be sensible about such things. No harm will come to you."

She grabbed up Amice's fallen gown, smoothed out the crumpled yellow taffeta. "It's not the best hue for your red colouring," she said, narrowing her eyes, "but it will have to do. And yes, the seamstress will need to adjust the bodice, just as Amice said. Your figure is much more…ripe…than hers."

She went to the door, calling for the local seamstress to be brought. I remained frozen like a statue, as a woman called Old Mattie came shuffling into the chamber, bent and wizened, so short sighted she could only see her needle and naught beyond. With mother guiding her in what needed to be done, they both began to fuss over my clothing.

As the dress went on, Mattie let it out in the front then sewed it taut again until my breasts strained outwards and upwards, jutting towards my chin. I felt like a prize heifer being readied for market. A cow with udders on display…just what Amice had called me during her angry outburst. "I am uncomfortable, Mother, I look like a harlot, a common whore!" I whined.

Mother's lips were thin lines. She nodded at Old Mattie with her deadly needle. "Tighter, Mattie, tighter. More lift. I have heard the King is attracted to…buxom women."

The needle darted in and out, shining silver. I gritted my teeth and struggled to breathe. Clearly, nothing I said or did would be to any avail.

The Great Hall was full of the household, the King's men, and guests from neighbouring castles and manors. Noise rose to shake the rafters. The central fire burned heartily, making the walls sweat; above my father's painted escutcheons the King's own banner, bearing a roaring lion, flapped and shimmered as if seeking to tear free of its fastenings and rampage about the room. All around the Hall warriors bragged and boasted, wearing on their breasts the badges of the King— an escarbuncle with eight protruding rods that terminated in Fleur de Lys, and the insignia of Henry's father's family, the Plantagenista, the golden sprig of broom. Servers were milling about, bearing dishes on the best plate; the smell of food mingled with the hot scent of the fire and the herbs mother had ordered scattered upon the mats.

The King sat next to my father on a gilded chair that he had brought in his baggage train; cleverly made, it folded up and down to be easily portable when he was on the road. Supported by graceful silver rods a canopy of estate was drawn over top of his seat; stars were picked out upon its surface in golden thread and the canopy itself was wrought of a soft, shining, dove-grey silk.

I sat with my two sisters on a bench running along the Hall's side, clad in Amice's stolen and now mutilated dress. She was still sulking, the corners of her lips down-turned in an unbecoming manner. I ignored her moping and glanced furtively at the King; he was deep in discussion with my father and did not seem to have noticed me.

Now, cleaned up and dressed for the feast, he looked far more regal than in the forest. He wore a long *bliaut* of blue silk from Andalusia in Spain, with the sleeves drawn tight to his elbows. Imported squirrel fur was sewn around cuffs and collar, a pale bluish-grey shade that went well with the Spanish silk. He wore no crown, but a golden band engraved with many designs.

As he raised a jewelled goblet to his lips, I heard the deep rumble of his voice while he spoke to my sire about the troubles with the Welsh: "You are one of the strongest of the Marcher Lords, Clifford. And one of the most hated after you had Einion Ap Anarawd murdered in his own bed."

"It was on the orders of Roger de Clare, Earl of Hertford." Father looked untroubled by being called a killer.

"But you were still his agent, were you not? And, so I've been told, all too happy to skewer the fellow."

Father shrugged and I breathed in sharply; I had not heard of father causing the death of anyone outside of honourable battle! "He was a traitor, my Lord King."

"Aye, you do not lie," Henry stroked his short, neat beard, "but Einion served me well enough at one time. And I would not gladly have Rhys Ap Gruffudd enraged any more than he normally is. Rhys was Einion's uncle."

"A lesson had to be taught, your Grace," said father firmly. "These Welshmen are savages. To be savage back towards them is all they understand."

"What about Cadwgan Ap Mareddudd?" asked Henry, taking another mouthful of wine. "You slew him too, did you not? Rhys demands vengeance for Cadwgan too, my lord of Clifford."

Father's lips tightened. "Yes, I did slay him. As the miscreant well deserved. He was with Rhys when they fell upon one of my castles several years back. They burnt it, your Grace! Burnt it after pillaging all its contents. I am just relieved my wife and daughters were not in it at the time…"

"Daughters." King Henry's head swung around. "Earlier you were telling me about them…How many? Three? Four?"

"Three. All young, all fair. Two are betrothed…but the eldest is not."

"Why? Is there something wrong with her?" asked the King, with a rather crass laugh.

"Not at all," said father. "She is a very special maid, of outstanding beauty. The kind minstrels sing about. I have debated whether to give her to God, to a house of nuns…"

"That would be a waste indeed if she is as fair as you say," murmured the King.

"Or to find a man suitable for such a one, who will give my daughter and her kin the honour they deserve. A man who will value the House of Clifford for the rare jewel he will receive."

My ears began to burn. I tried to turn my attention away to a dwarf dancing around in a corner of the Hall, flipping over the back of a weary-looking greyhound. The dwarf winked at me, wiggled his arse in a lewd fashion.

"Do you like music, my liege?" I heard father ask the King. "I have fine musicians for your pleasure. My daughters may dance for you, if it be your will."

Henry chuckled. "I would never say no to the sight of fair maidens dancing, Lord Clifford."

Father climbed to his feet, beckoning to me, Amice, Lucie and the other women and men gathered in the Great Hall. Reluctantly I took my place, partnered with a young squire of good blood called Medgel. We began a swift circle dance, as the leader of the women, Bertha Fitzwalter, the heiress wife of the Marcher lord William de Braose, sang out the words of the rather bawdy song:

"Tis the joyful season, O maidens!
Come hence you young men and rejoice!
O! O! My heart is all a-flower!
My body's burning at the thought of first love,
I have a bright new love that spells my doom!
The nightingale, she sings so sweetly;
Her melody sets my blood on fire.
O! O! My heart is all a-flower!
My body's burning at the thought..."

We twirled, circled, bowed and curtseyed; Medgel's sweaty hand was clamped firmly on mine. Amidst the whirling and swirling, I saw Henry in his high seat, watching with full attentiveness. He leant forward , his gaze fixed upon me. Emotion shone in his eyes, and yet…yet…to my wonderment, it was not the naked lust I had seen in the forest, the raw urge to mate. Desire of fleshly things, perhaps, but definitely something more than that…Confusion? Surprise?

I wanted to watch the King more closely, but I dared not make my interest too visible, and besides, I was drawn into the circle again, being swept round and round, Medgel's blunt-cut yellow hair blowing back into my flushed face.

A knight surnamed de Montmorency took the hand of Bertha Fitzwalter, and as they stood before the lord's dais, in a resounding baritone he continued with the song of first love and first desire.

"My fair love is a virgin among virgins
And a rose among roses.
O! O! My heart is all a-flower!
My body's burning at the thought...
Your consent comforts me,
While your refusal exiles me.
O! O! My heart is all a-flower...
My body's burning...."

The dance ended. Father grabbed me by the arm, his eyes shining. His breath was hot and ripe with the scent of the spices in his wine "You did well, Rosamund. He wants to speak with you. Remember, say nothing foolish to make him turn away."

I made no response. The world was blurring around me, made torturous from too many sensations; heat from the fire, the flash of torches, the smell of sweat and perfumes and dogs and food. I fought to keep control of my head and my trembling legs as my father guided me before the King.

"So you are the Fair Rosamund," he smiled down at me. "You look a little different...now that you are less wet!"

"Your Grace." I dropped a deep curtsey. "I hope I did not offend upon that day. It was not my intention."

"It was I who offended, not you," said Henry. "I behaved like a boor. I did not expect my host's daughter to be...well...unescorted in a wood. I did not know who you were."

"And I was ignorant of your Grace's identity too," I said.

"So all will be forgiven on both sides." Henry's eyes gleamed. "We will start...anew."

Uncertain how to respond, I stared at the rush-laden floor. His words haunted me...*We will start*....

"Would you dance with me?" The King's huge, sword-calloused hand stretched in my direction. He asked a question, but I knew there was only one answer he would accept.

"I would be honoured, your Grace." My voice emerged a high-pitched squeak.

We danced. People gawked. The minstrel yowled like a stepped-on cat. The hurdy gurdy whirred. Father grinned like a madman. King Henry stood close, too close, to me, smiling. Heat radiated from him, hot as the fire.

And then it was over. "Sit near me," he ordered.

A chair was brought, and then platters of candied figs and frumenty and a subtlety of checked azure and gold—our family's arms displayed in confectionary. Henry spoke to me of many things—his fine horses, his love of books, Normandy and Anjou, his father Geoffrey le Bel the Fair, and even his fierce mother Empress Maud. He spoke to me of the legends of King Arthur, which were popular amongst the Norman lords as well as the Welsh, and of his desire for the conquest of Wales. The Welsh would come to heel…when he had dealt with them; so too would the Irish fall. I was rather surprised he spoke with such candour to a mere maiden…and I found myself liking him for it. Father never spoke to us of any of his business. He did not even involve mother in his affairs.

The banquet ended. The King turned from me back to my sire and began to talk in earnest about masculine subjects—the raising of levies, the strengthening of castles, the best strategic moves his army might take against the crafty Welsh. The banquet-goers began filing out of the Great Hall, nodding in satisfaction as they made for their waiting bedchambers.

My tiring women and nurses hustled me from the hall along with Amice and Lucie. Amice was sullen, seeming to have realised the intent of father's ploy, but Lucie, as ever, was chattering like a little bird, the excitement of the night overwhelming her. "The King…he danced so well! And he spoke to you for so long, Rosamund. How lucky you are!"

"Am I?" I murmured, but I found I was smiling slightly. Yes, I was. Henry was not nearly as fearsome as I expected. The more I looked into his face and heard his speech, the more charming I found him. Despite his large head and short limbs, women called him handsome…and now I could understand why…

The archway leading to the bedchamber I shared with my siblings loomed before me, the oak door gaping open wide. Suddenly, my nurses thrust me inside, while my sisters, protesting in alarm, were propelled on down the corridor.

The door shut behind me with a soft but final thud. I found myself alone with nurse Mildred, an old woman I feared and despised. She had been my father's nurse when he was a boy, so she was a very great age indeed. She was bad tempered and scarcely able to work anymore with her physical complaints, but my father clearly had some affection for the woman and saw that she never went without. She had once been a skilled herbalist, as well as a midwife; I heard father also used to employ her as a spy when he needed to know about goings-on in the village.

Mildred wore a dark, floor-length robe, not unlike a nun's, wrapped so tightly around her bony limbs she resembled a shrouded corpse. Her small, mean eyes flicked in sunken hollows.

"I have stoked up the fire….despite the pain of my rheumatism." She gestured to the hearth with a claw-like hand. "And I had some comforts brought." She nodded toward the bed, its usual plain cover gone and replaced with an exquisite silk quilt. A bowl of rose water for laving the hands and face stood next to it, and bundles of sweet smelling herbs dangled from the bed-frame.

I stood motionless, not knowing what to say or do. Though the King had turned back to father at the end of our discourse, it was clear old Mildred—and hence my sire—expected his imminent arrival. King Henry would surely want his 'gift.'

Mildred clicked her tongue disapprovingly. "Don't just stand there gaping, Lady Rosamund. This may be the most important night of your life. Put a smile on your face! Look winsome and welcoming!"

My old fears flooded back and a little moan broke from the back of my throat. My eyes began to tear.

"None of that weeping now!" admonished Mildred, her near-lipless and toothless mouth stern. "It will make you look unattractive. No man wants to see a red face and eyes—especially a King."

"Don't you understand, Mildred?" I gulped, trying to control my emotions. "I don't want him to admire me. I hardly know him. He is not my wedded husband. I will only be a mistress, a concubine, and not a lawfully wedded wife."

Mildred heaved a great, despairing sigh. "You should be honoured by his attentions. Most girls would be. As for not knowing him; well, even if you were being wed, there is a good chance you would not have met your husband until the wedding day."

She shuffled up to me, smelling of age, rank flesh and the potions she brewed. She thrust a phial of liquid into my hands. "Drink this, Lady, and be quick about it …it contains asafoetida and pennyroyal. It should hopefully prevent you from becoming with child, although such things are never certain."

I took the phial, my hands shaking. A child! I had scarcely even thought of such a possibility. I thought I might be sick but watched by Mildred, I forced myself to down her potion, grimacing at both taste and smell.

It was for the best, I told myself. And perhaps it would turn out it was not even needed. Maybe he would not come tonight. Maybe the King would drink himself into a stupor with his men.

"Let me ready you for bed." Mildred pulled at the lacing on my gown. "Quick, girl…help me, my old fingers are bent and stiff!"

Embarrassed, I slipped out of my fine gown and stood shivering on the flagstones clad only in my long red hair. Grumbling, Mildred went to the wooden chest at the end of the bed, pulled out my white linen nightgown and dragged it over my head.

"There." She looked satisfied with herself as she arranged my hair over my shoulders. "My job here tonight is done. May God smile on you, Lady Rosamund. And his Grace too, of course!""

Mildred shuffled from the bedchamber and I curled up on the bed under the exquisite coverlet. Despite the fire burning in the brazier, I was trembling as my body touched the bleached sheets. The smell of lavender and other herbs scattered about reached into my nostrils, making me feel rather giddy and ill.

Did I pray to Blessed Mary that he didn't come to me? She was a virgin, after all. There were armies of virgin saints too, many of whom took their lives rather than succumb to the embrace of an unwanted lover…

But…I did not want to die. I was no saint. And I had a sire who was also no saint. Would it go the worse for me if Henry did not desire me? Would I be blamed, maybe with dire consequences?

I did not know how I should think, and after a while, despite my apprehension, I began to drowse off.

I awoke in darkness; the tallow candle on the ledge nearest the bed had burnt down. The fire was still going but had been reduced to red embers. Coldness bit into me; goose bumps lining my arms, I slipped out of the bed to stoke the failing flames.

As I knelt on the woven mat before the hearth, there was a sound, a soft footfall in the corridor beyond. A gasp tore from my lips, as the door to my chamber opened and King Henry stepped inside.

I dropped the poker I clasped in my hand and sought to rise and curtsey before my sovereign.

"Stop! You may stay where you are!" The King walked slowly towards me.

He smiled down, firelight playing over his distinctive features and stroking the strong jaw line, sparking the fire in his thick, cropped hair. "But I would appreciate if you put the poker down, Rosamund. Were you planning to stab me with it?"

"Oh, oh, no…of course not, my Lord King! I would never dare raise my hand against your Grace." I dropped the poker with a metallic clang and it rolled away into the darkness.

Henry stood staring at me as if entranced. "That is good to hear, Rosamund Clifford. But I wish you would indeed raise your fair white hand to me…though not in anger, but in the caress of a lover."

He was clad just in a long night-robe; forest-green velvet embroidered with little roaring lions in gold. I saw it gap as he took a step in my direction, caught a brief glimpse of compact, muscled limbs.

I blushed and glanced away, mortified. Henry bent over and caught hold of both my wrists in a firm but gentle grip, drawing me to my feet. I was suddenly aware that the firelight was shining straight through the thin fabric of my voluminous nightdress. He seemed aware of it also. All too aware. His gaze travelled down the length of me, approving. I heard his breathing deepen.

Henry's hand reached to cup my chin, tilting my face up to his. "I think you are a witch, Rose of the World. You have enchanted me."

"Oh, do not say so, your Grace. Witchcraft is evil!" Women were often blamed for the bad actions of men because of their supposed 'witchery'. I did not want that stigma. I did not weave spells or pray to the moon to make the King or anyone else my lover. I had not looked to have any man as my paramour.

"You are a nymph then. A wild forest spirit…as I first saw you. Were you about to divest yourself of your garb that day and dance naked upon the greensward?"

"I would never dream of such a thing!" I was aware of his hand, having left my face, running across my buttocks up to the small of my back, pressing me closer to him.

"Well, tonight you will dance for me, Rosamund Clifford."

The hands left my back, raced to the neck of my night robe. As if it were mere flimsy tissue, he tore it open neck to ankle. A gasp of fear and yet excitement came from my mouth; he stifled the sound with his mouth, his lips hard against mine, his tongue exploring the edges of my teeth. Fingers darted over my flesh, seeking, exploring, playing me like an instrument.

"Rosamund…" The King's voice was a primal growl. Suddenly tearing his lips from mine, he stepped back a pace and grasped the arm of my torn, fluttering nightgown. Pulling the tattered rag from my body, he balled it up and cast it upon the embers of the fire. After a second, the thin cloth caught alight and burst into bright, dancing flames.

Henry laughed as sparks spiralled upwards, and then he wrapped his strong arms around me and lifted me from my feet, carrying me to the bed.

He set me down on the coverlet; I lay like some ancient maiden sacrifice, like the Green Lady that legend said was buried beneath the tower—my red hair flowing outwards in a gleaming wheel of russet tendrils, my white limbs stretched out, naked and wanton, chilled and yet burning at the core, waiting for the life I knew to end with one unchangeable deed…

Henry reached to his waist and undid the cord that held his robe fast. Dropping it, he stood before me like some ancient god of fertility, powerful and terrible, compelling and terrifying, limned in the red light of the fire.

I gazed at him, my eyes wide…and suddenly I began to weep.

I did not intend to and hated myself even as tears rolled aimlessly down my cheeks. I was not a child; I should not behave so!

Henry frowned and fear leapt into my heart. "Your Grace!" I cried, and my voice was as shrill as the wind that blew around the castle. "I did not mean to upset you. Please do not be angry with me. If I do not please you, my father will…"

I shut my mouth with a snap; Henry's eyes were glittering dangerously.

"Your father will do exactly what?" he growled. "Beat you?"

"Maybe," I said weakly, my bare shoulders sagging.

Henry made a disgusted noise and pulled his robe back on with jerky, frustrated motions. I rolled over, onto my knees, my hair falling in a cloak to hide my nakedness. "My Lord King?"

"If I were younger…" Henry went over to the ewer with the rosewater, splashing some on his florid face, "I would have paid no heed to a virgin's tears, and gone on to take what I desire. I am not as young now, and have more sense. I want more than just a pretty face and inviting paps. You are too young and unsophisticated for me as yet, Rosamund Clifford, even as a temporary diversion. And…" he suddenly smiled, "your qualities enamour me enough to believe you might be worth more than just a night's play. But only time will tell. Therefore, my Lady, I bid you goodnight and farewell."

He leaned over to assail my mouth with one final kiss, and then, with a small, disappointed sigh, left my chamber.

Cold with dismay, I lay on the bed. I had caused the King to reject me. He was gone.

Confused tears started again. They only stopped when I saw something lying on the coverlet, gleaming blood red in the fire's dimming glow.

Henry Plantagenet, King of England, had left me a gift—a fat ruby that must have been worth a fortune. A ruby the colour of a ripe red rose.

I picked the gemstone up and gazed at my tear-streaked face reflected a dozen times within its crimson facets.

The next day the King left Clifford Castle with much fanfare; I did not watch him depart, nor did he send a message. I was not sure whether to be glad or sorrowful that he was gone.

My sisters returned to share the bedchamber, something we had always done, but to my dismay, I found they treated me differently to before. It was almost as if a magician's wand had passed over me in one fatal night, changing me from plain Rosamund...to something else. *Someone* else, a stranger. A stranger who might be slightly unsavoury, who had secrets never to be divulged. Even Lucie's usual ebullience was muted; no questions were asked and rather than converse with me, she busied herself with her embroidery, which had never amused her much before.

Father's manner was perplexing too. I had expected anger...for surely he knew that the King had not spent the night in my bed, but he said nothing. He wore a hard little smile, however, as he embarked on the King's business in preparation for his incursion into Wales, which was planned for later that year.

I was like a phantom, walking the halls of Clifford Castle.

Then mother went into her confinement, and after a hard labour that nearly killed her was delivered of a healthy son, whom father named Gilbert. The drama of the moment took the attention from me as we all gathered in the castle chapel to pray that mother would live.

She did, though she remained extremely weak, while despite a hard birth the baby thrived, howling like a little demon when he was Christened, the water from the font splashing over his bald head. Once mother was churched, the required forty days having passed, father announced that it was time for Amice to leave Clifford Castle and join her betrothed, Osbern FitzHugh, at his stronghold at Richard's Castle. Amice was delighted, enjoying being the centre of attention in the household instead of taking a back seat as the 'quiet sensible one' wedged between two more temperamental sisters.

"I shall be so happy to marry Osbern," she cooed, while servants packed her trousseau and filled chests with linens and dresses. "It will be hard to leave Clifford Castle, but Richard's Castle in not so far away that I cannot visit. Maybe you will be able to visit me...and my children." She beamed as if she were already with child and not a bride-to-be who had only met her betrothed once or twice.

"I would wager Osbern will have grown a full hand taller since last you laid eyes on him," I said, injecting a hint of reality into my sister's moonstruck conversation. Osbern, as I remembered him, was a short and weedy boy, immature in nature, who had no interests other than hawks and hounds. "I wonder if his pimples have cleared up?"

Amice pouted. "I am sure they have. I am sure he is an upright, and handsome, Marcher lord."

"It's a pity you won't be there to see, Rosamund..." began Lucie, stitching merrily away at her embroidery...then she fumbled, looked embarrassed, and yelled 'Ow' as she stabbed her thumb with the needle.

"Lucie, what do you mean?" A cold sensation washed over me.

"N...nothing," Lucie stammered. "I should have said nothing."

I glanced at Amice; guiltily she stared down at the flagstones. "Don't lie to me!" I cried. "You both know something I don't! Why would I not see Amice's wedding?"

Lucie bit her lip; her thumb was bleeding all over her stitching. "It...it...We heard father talking, Amice and me. By accident. He was talking about what he wanted for you. Rosamund, he wants to send you away..."

"Away where?" My voice dropped to a whisper.

"South," said Amice. And then she bowed her head, "To a nunnery."

"A...a nunnery!" My face flamed. "I know it is an honour to serve God but I have no calling..." My head began to spin and I leant against the wall. So this would be my punishment for displeasing the King and my father. I had remained a virgin and now I would remain so forever, locked within the sterns walls of the cloister.

"I cannot bear this!" I cried, and with my face buried in my hands, I ran from the bedchamber like a mad thing, seeking my mother's quarters.

Despite the impropriety, especially when mother had been so ill after baby Gilbert's birth, I burst into the chamber unannounced and flung myself at her feet. "Please don't make me be a nun!" I cried. "I beg you, Lady Mother, intercede for me with father. Allow me to stay at Clifford Castle; I swear I will be no trouble to you!"

Mother's wan face relaxed after her initial surprise. She stroked my curls with long fingers. "Rosamund, Rosamund, what have you heard? Your father has decided to send you to a convent, yes...but not to be a nun. As you know, a young woman can get a decent education with the sisters. You can learn far more in a convent than in Clifford Castle. We do the best we can here with tutors for you but we are very provincial. That may be fine for your younger sisters…but not for an elder daughter."

"I can embroider well enough, and I know the Lord's Prayer."

"In a convent, you will have access to great books, holy books, important books that impart knowledge. You will learn Latin, you will improve your reading and writing skills, you will continue to study the arts of sewing and spinning. You will learn about plants that heal and harm, and when to plant them and harvest them. Your court French will be much improved and you will sing plainsong to the glory of God. You may even learn to cook, as the Benedictine nuns make their own food and do not hire outsiders to cook for them. You will be virtuous…until the time comes…"

"The time comes for what?" I asked mutinously.

"Till your father comes to an arrangement for you," said mother, somewhat offhandedly. She suddenly turned and beckoned to her maid. "Emma, will you bring some watered-down wine? My stomach feels queasy."

Emma cast me a dark look as if she believed I were responsible for my mother's distress and reached for a pitcher of wine on the table. Perhaps I was selfish, mother's lips looked bloodless and drawn and her hands shook, but I could not stop myself from speaking.

"This…this is unfair!" I stammered, my hands curling into tight fists. "Father acted as a...a procurer for the King, and while that did not go as planned, now he wants me primped and prepared…for *what*? For who? Well, I won't have it! Maybe I will go into this convent he has chosen and seek to take holy orders there."

Mother nearly dropped the goblet Emma had handed to her. "Rosamund! When did you grow so wilful, so disobedient? How could you think of such a thing! Do not go against your father's will! A dutiful daughter should respect her parents' wishes!"

"What will he do if I decide to marry God instead of whatever horrible man he might dig up for me?" I sneered, unable to hold back my insolence, despite the fact it was not my mother's fault. I hated both my parents, in that instant—father for using me as a pawn, mother for going along with his wishes like a timid sheep. "Will he bring his men to attack the nuns? Well, he is rather free with his use of the sword, is he not? He has a hateful reputation here in the Marcher-lands."

"His reputation, as you put it, is what keeps you safe at night!" Mother stared at me, tears standing in her eyes. And a kind of fear. A fear of what? Father? "Please," she begged again, "do not cross him. Walter is not a man you want to cross."

"I am guessing you learnt that long ago," I said with bitterness. "How else would a woman of your rank end up with someone like him?"

"You must not speak of it! He would thrash you if he heard such venomous talk!" Mother's voice rose, tremulous; she clutched the jewelled cross she wore around her neck. "Ah, Emma, I feel most faint…"

"Lady Rosamund, you must go now!" Emma was positively scowling, her brows like thunder as she fanned my mother's ashen face.

My bravado was waning; after my initial harsh words, guilt bit at me—I did not truly want to distress my mother, not after the difficult birth she had recently suffered. No doubt, she had other sorrows to bear too, as the wife of hard-handed Walter Clifford.

"Mother, forgive me, I did not seek to distress you but I am so troubled in mind…" I said.

"Go, go…it does not matter; you are forgiven." Mother waved a limp hand, gesturing me towards the chamber door. She choked on her wine; redness emerged from the corners of her mouth and dribbled down her chin. How pathetic and weak she looked; Margaret de Tosney, who was related to great lords and even kings, who had once in her youth been acclaimed as a great beauty. "Go, Rosamund, but swear to me you will not defy your father in this matter. If you must battle the world, choose a battle you can win! This one you cannot—so swear!"

Dull-eyed, I bit my lip. She was correct; I might scream defiance until the towers shook but I could never sway father once he had embarked upon a course of action. "I swear," I whispered in a quavering voice. "For you, mother, I do swear."

And so I departed the castle where I had grown up, heading for the convent at Godstow, which stood several miles outside the town of Oxford. Amice and Lucie waved me farewell but would not meet my eyes as I rode through the gate on my palfrey. Mother did not come to say farewell; afflicted by a pounding head, so she said, she had taken to her bed. Father was too busy elsewhere, helping prepare men and supplies for the King's forthcoming incursion into Wales.

As the cavalcade travelled south towards Oxfordshire, I took note of the preparations for invasion in every town we passed; armed men moving down the muddy roads, supply carts groaning beneath heavy loads. I wondered if the King was nearby, taking charge of the situation as Henry FitzEmpress always did—with speed and efficiency.

After several tedious days of travel, during which we stopped at friendly manors and monastic houses for the night, my party came within sight of Oxford. Excitement rushed through me; the largest town I had ever visited till now was Hereford and it was dwarfed by Oxford, one of the biggest towns in England. As we approached, hundreds upon hundreds of spires of golden stone sprang into a blood-red evening sky, and I could hear the clanging of dozens of church and abbey bells.

My father's man, Gervaise de Telfer, turned to me, a looming figure in mail upon the back of a grey stallion. "We will enter the town for the night, Lady Rosamund. A messenger from Godstow will meet us there, at the Augustinian house of St Frideswide. On the morrow, when all are refreshed, we will set out on the last leg of the journey to Godstow."

We entered Oxford by crossing Small Bridge and Bookbinder's Bridge, and passed in silence along the frowning outer wall of the castle. I stared up at the stern grey walls, mirrored in the darkening swell of the stream that sucked at their stony feet. On occasion, King Henry stayed there at the apartments he retained within; years ago, during the Anarchy, when his mother, Empress Maud, fought King Stephen for supremacy, she escaped the besieged castle by darting across the frozen river in a white cowl, while a blizzard raged around her and siege engines hurled missiles at the castle defences.

The town was much more peaceable now, if not exactly quiet; even at this late hour, it buzzed with life. Students from the colleges swarmed through the streets and the taverns were merry, torchlight spilling from windows and doors. De Telfer, looking stern, beckoned to my father's men to gather close to my mount and the two servants sent to wait on me.

As I saw his hand reach to his sword hilt, I lifted my brows in surprise. "I am sure it will not come to that, Sir Gervaise. Surely Oxford is a decent place, with its scholars and churches? What ruffian would dare attack our entourage in the middle of a busy street?"

Gervaise smiled grimly. "Alas, my Lady, any place where many men dwell close together is subject to disharmony. The common men of the town and the scholars frequently war…and ofttimes break each others' heads. But do not fear, I will allow no harm to come to you."

We journeyed on, faring through towered Westgate, where the watch waved us in immediately, then past the tall bastion of St Aldate's church and across Fishmonger's street to St Frideswide's priory.

The priory was small and not as impressive as I had hoped it might be, and the streets around were thronged with noisy students, since several of the colleges stood in the vicinity. Frideswide was Oxford's own patron saint, but it seems the house dedicated to her, set as it was in the heart of Oxford's bustle, was not particularly conducive to quiet contemplation and prayer.

Inside the courtyard, we were met by the Prior, Robert of Cricklade, a genial older man who made us welcome. With him was a young nun clad in grey robes of undyed wool—Sister Hosanna from Godstow, our guide for the morrow. "I will let Sister Hosanna take you to your quarters, Lady Rosamund," said the Prior cheerfully. "I am sure after your wanderings in the wild you will be needing rest, water and refreshments. All shall be provided, of course; we pride ourselves on hospitality at St Frideswide's. I myself must hasten back to work, though, alas. I am writing a book!"

"A book, how marvellous," I said, remembering my manners, although I truly had no interest in the Prior's hobbies. "Is it about the good saint Frideswide?"

"Indeed it is….but she is not the only subject I am interested in. I have written other books too—one about Jacob and an Anthology of Pliny's Natural History. I have dedicated the latter to the King!"

I flushed then, turning my face away from Prior Robert in case he could read my guilt, see the sin in my heart. He gave his sovereign a book…What had I almost given him?

"Whether he will ever read my little work…" The Prior shrugged, giving a wry little smile. "Although he may. It is true that he likes books, despite his roistering and womanising. A man of contradictions."

My colour deepened further and I stared down at my feet, playing the part of an innocent maid much embarrassed by the mention of the King's proclivities. Not one who had lain naked in his arms…even if nothing more had happened and her virtue was unblemished.

Sister Hosanna must have realised my discomfort for she coughed loudly and said, "I will take you to your chamber. You look exhausted, you poor dear…" She seemed greatly interested in me and behind closed doors began a joyous chatter about life at Godstow. To my relief, it sounded as if the nuns there were kindly and interested in the world beyond their walls; some of them taught local children, and many travellers stayed at the priory as they passed in and out of Oxford on their journeys.

Hosanna was the twelfth daughter of a minor Berkshire knight; he had promised his youngest girl to the church if God would finally smile down and give him a son. God did, with the aid of the knight's long-suffering lady, of course, and so, dragging a paltry dowry with her, Hosanna was sent to Godstow.

"Were you glad to become a nun?" I asked shyly.

"Quite," she replied. "I didn't want my mother's life, bearing children each year and being blamed when no boys were forthcoming! I never met a man I would contemplate marrying; oafish, violent, lustful...I saw all of that amongst my father's friends and it repelled me. Christ will be my only groom until death. What of you, Lady Rosamund? I know you are with the sisters to receive your education rather than to take the veil….but would you consider taking orders should you find a calling?"

I moved uneasily about the tiny room; a star was shining through the high slit of the window, casting silverish light over the cold tiles with their patterns of lions and leaves. The lions made me think of King Henry; he sometimes used one upon his standard. "I had not thought about it if I am honest. I…I think my father will want marriage for me, but he keeps his plans to himself. But who knows, Sister Hosanna; none can say what fate will bring us."

"No, that is true…only God knows that, of course. For instance, I am sure the Lady Ediva, wife of Sir William Lanceline, did not know she would be called by the Almighty to found the priory at Godstow. After her husband's death, she had been living as a hermitess near the Holy Well of Binsey, sacred to both St Margaret and St Frideswide, the foundress of this great House, blessed be her name. While praying one night, Ediva heard a mighty voice calling out and telling her to build a church where the light from heaven touched the ground. She wandered from her hermit's cell. and following the banks of the Thames, came upon an island amid the churning waters. As she gazed upon it, the sun broke through the clouds and a spear of light descended to strike a hummock in the centre of the island. It was Easter, and her quest was over."

Her quest was over…I almost envied that long dead nun, pious and holy, her future clear in her own mind. My quest, my journey, was just beginning, and I did not even know what it would be. Saintly, sensible, sinful…I had no idea.

Sister Hosanna moved over to her hard sleeping pallet at the foot of my slightly less uncomfortable bed. She lay down; like most nuns, she slept in her habit. "Well, the hour is growing late; we had best seek some sleep. Godstow is not far from Oxford but it will be a busy day for you, Lady Rosamund, and no doubt wearying if you have not had proper rest. I bid you good night."

I called my two servants to undress me; other than tomorrow morn, it was the last time such personal attention would be needed. After I had been delivered to Godstow, the servants would return with the rest of the party to the Marches. They were tearful, fluttering around me as they tried to come up with positive aspects of convent life to cheer me.

Then they were gone, scurrying to their own quarters in the stables, and I was left with my little guide Hosanna, who was already snoring on her pallet. The walk from Godstow to meet my party must have tired her out…and the bare, calloused feet sticking off the end of the pallet were crusted with dirt.

Climbing into my bed, I tried to sleep but outside the walls of the priory of Saint Frideswide, I could hear the students of Oxford singing drunkenly as they milled from tavern to tavern in the fog rising from the river Isis—

"Ama me fideliter,
fidem meam nota,
de corde totaliter
et ex mente tota,
sum presentialiter
alens in remota;
quisquis amat taliter,
volvitur in rota."

I had some decent knowledge of Latin, and the words struck me deep, filling me with strange, nameless longing:
Love me with fidelity,
Taking heed of my loyalty,
With all your heart,
With all your mind.
I am closest to you

When I am far away;
Whoever loves like this
Rides on Fortune's Wheel.

Though the night was not cold, I began to shiver. With a brisk motion, I dragged the coverlet up round my ears to stop the sound of the scholars' singing.

We reached Godstow Priory shortly after noon the next day, Sister Hosanna leading the party and pointing out landmarks upon the way. Sure enough, as she had described, the priory stood upon an island between two swift-moving streams that fed into the Thames. Made of local limestone, the spire of the church and the outer walls glowed pale in the unbroken sunlight. Birds were wheeling in off the river to settle along the graceful roofline with its statues and finials, their voices sharp and lonely above the ceaseless rush of the water.

We rode to the gatehouse, a stout two-storied building with a bell swaying above the door and statuary of the Virgin and John the Baptist in niches. A large gate gapped open for the passage of carts, while beside it was a low, rounded arch where travellers on foot would enter. To my surprise, Hosanna told me that the road to Wolvercote ran straight through the outer courtyard; this brought an odd sense of relief—at least I could hear news brought by passersby seeking lodgings at the priory and not be completely shut off from the world.

I dismounted my horse and handed the reins over to Gervaise de Telfer. She'd been a good horse but she would return to Clifford Castle; maybe Lucie would have her. The meagre belongings that I had been permitted to bring were being unloaded from the cart by servants of the priory and carried away. I suspected most of them would not be seen again.

Hosanna tugged shyly on my sleeve. "Come, Lady Rosamund. The Prioress Edith will be awaiting you. She does not like to be kept waiting, as her day is always so busy."

I took a deep breath. My new life had begun.

Life was pleasant enough at Godstow but it was certainly not exciting. I told myself such dullness was for the best, and it was good to be away from father's machinations. Back home at Clifford Castle, I would no longer even have Amice to rely on for support, since she was now wedded to the spotty-cheeked Osbern and mistress of her own household.

Dressed in grey woollen like the nuns themselves, my hair modestly covered by a coif, I worked with the local village children and was given great tomes to study to expand my knowledge of things both religious and secular. Sister Hosanna coached me on my Latin, in which I soon grew proficient. Readily, I learned herb-lore and how to treat the sick with various remedies. Prioress Edith counselled me on running an estate, showing me how to keep ledgers to tally the costs and running through the lists of food, supplies and servants I would need to keep a household prosperous. Sometimes I learned so much my head hurt with it all.

Despite being of decent birth, I was kept as humble as those women who had taken orders and scrubbed and cleaned just as they did. I swept out the priest's lodging and polished the candlesticks in St Thomas's chapel, where the nun's small staff of servants went to pray, separate from the nuns, who used the priory church for their devotions. I bundled herbs, dried them, hung them up and I aided in the laundry when needed, despite the steam reddening my face and the water wrinkling my hands.

I quite enjoyed being busy, as it kept me from thinking. Thinking of my future. And thinking of *him*. The King.

Sitting alongside the sisters at table, where we ate our meagre but wholesome fare, I often felt isolated and strange, wondering if the others ever felt the…longings I did. Longings that they, sisters in Christ, would deem immoral. But I was different from them. I was not there to take vows; I was not a novitiate or postulant, not even an oblate. One day, I would leave Godstow and be wed to whomever my father commanded.

Time passed. Boredom grew. I began to linger around the priory courtyard when travellers came for respite, hoping to hear news of far away places and see unfamiliar faces. Most who came to Godstow were burly merchants heading to Oxford, their carts groaning under the weight of their wares and their rude servants eyeing me and some of the other sisters with ill-disguised lust…but then one day the Wolvercote road was full of men. Men in armour, men on horses. Banners flew and clarions shrilled, their sound making the river birds soar off in great clouds.

Rushing to the gate with Hosanna and a postulant called Mabella, we watched as contingents of heavily armed soldiers marched in the direction of the palace of Woodstock.

"I don't like the look of this!" whispered Mabella, cheeks pale against her stark wimple. "I hope war isn't coming. My father told me many dreadful tales of the battles between King Stephen and Empress Matilda. It was said God and his saints slept in those evil times."

"Don't be foolish, Mabella," said Hosanna. "Those times are over and done. King Henry is a mighty lord and would crush any rebellion…" she made a crushing motion with her hand, "with a mailed fist!"

"Look!" I could not contain myself, pointing to the banner borne proudly down the middle of the line. The lion! Henry's lion. "Whatever is happening, it *is* something to do with his Grace the King! I must go and see!"

Ignoring Hosanna and Mabella's shouts, I propelled myself from the priory gate and onto the road.

Spearmen and archers grinned, winked; I ignored them and approached a knight seated upon a powerful black stallion; he wore the device of de Camville, a known supporter of the King. "My lord," I cried, gazing up at him. "What news? Why do so many march towards Woodstock upon this day?"

The knight glanced down with a bemused smile. "You're an inquisitive little nun, aren't you? Should you not be off at your prayers?"

"I beg you for information, my lord. Should men march to war, we must know if our doors should be barred."

"I only jested with you, little nun," said the knight. "We ride for Woodstock to attend a great council. The King has been in Wales, quelling rebellion."

"And what has been the result of his endeavours?"

The man grinned. "The Welsh princes Rhys and Owain ap Gruffydd have agreed to come to Woodstock. There they will pay homage to Henry's son, Young Henry, who will one day be made King of England. Malcolm of Scotland will also attend for this purpose; he will leave his brother David as a hostage for his good behaviour."

I gasped. "So…the..the King…He will be nearby?"

"Where else would he be, little nun?" laughed the man, shaking his head as if he deemed me a witless ninny.

And then, turning his attention to matters more pressing than talking to a girl, he flicked his reins over his stallion's neck and vanished amidst the sea of banners and shields, while Hosanna darted out and hauled me back through the priory gate. Clutching my arm, she almost dragged me across the courtyard. "Those soldiers…they were looking at you sinfully," she hissed into my ear as we entered the safety of the cloister.

I did not tell her my own thoughts led in a sinful direction, as I thought of Henry King of England, so near to me at Woodstock…and yet surely unaware of my proximity. Or that I thought of him.

Time marched on, as it always must, just like the stout warriors massed at the gate. Wales had unexpectedly risen against Henry; Rhys Ap Gruffudd had broken his truce as well as his recent oaths to Young Henry, which was no surprise, for Henry was but an eight-year-old boy when the Welsh prince grudgingly did homage on his knees before him.

Rhys stormed Cantref Mawr and the stalwart castle of Dinefwr, and his vast hosts of Welshmen threatened to cut off Carmarthen, with its important fortress, once used by the Romans. Aberystwyth was overwhelmed and ransacked and flames leapt over Mabwynion and Ceredigion. The migrant Flemings who had settled nearby with permission from the King were driven out and their homes and businesses put to the torch by the angry Welshmen.

The nuns tutted at such unhappy tales and prayed to Our Lady for the safety of the poor Flemings, foreigners though they were.

I prayed, in secret, for the safety of the King, who was rumoured to be enraged to the point of madness by Rhys' perfidy. That was not the only thing to vex him in that cold, rainy, troubled year. He fell afoul of his good friend, Thomas Becket, Archbishop of Canterbury. Once they had diced and dined together, hunted and hawked in perfect amity…Now a rift had grown between them, threatening to stretch into a chasm.

Originally, Henry had given the position of Archbishop to Thomas in the hopes that it would draw the church closer to the crown;

his plan failed and, instead, the appointment divided them. Angrily, Henry accused Becket of appropriating £300 when he was Lord Chancellor and ordered him tried at Northampton castle. Becket strenuously denied any wrongdoing but offered to pay the missing money to the King nonetheless, which made many believe he was guilty—before his peers he was convicted of theft and of undermining royal authority. When the barons began to bandy about the dreaded word 'treason', Thomas Becket fled in fear to France. It was a great scandal, an Archbishop driven out by a King.

"I cannot believe Archbishop Becket has fled." Hosanna shook her head in dismay as we walked together through the cloisters of Godstow. "What is the country coming to, with the Welsh burning out the Flemings and wrecking the King's castles, and the King threatening the Archbishop? He spoke of charging him with treason…You know what that would mean if the Archbishop were found guilty?"

Despite knowing but little of the feud, I was strangely protective of Henry. "Becket must have acted inappropriately towards his Grace to fall from favour in this fashion. Most probably, he grew too proud and abused his position. A position given him by the King!"

"But the Archbishop of Canterbury is a great, holy man," argued Hosanna, aghast at my lack of respect for the exiled Becket. "The King…well, I know he's the King, and is above other men because of that, but…but…"

"But what?" My eyes narrowed.

"He…he can be of vile temper. They say he chews the rushes on the floor when in a rage! And that is not all. He is guilty…of the sin of concupiscence. Not only did he marry a woman so unclean his own father is said to have bedded her, he had been in and out of beds all over England and France!"

"What would you, a nun, know about beds and what goes on in them?" I snapped, wanting this horrible talk to end. *You don't know what I do, Hosanna…*

Hosanna ignored the coldness in my voice. "Some say he has eight illegitimate children with a whore called Ykenai; for sure, he has at least one child by her, Geoffrey FitzRoy, whom he has acknowledged as his own."

"He seems chaste compared to his grandfather, Henry One, who seemed to get a dozen byblows every moon," I quipped. "Really, Hosanna…Prioress Edith would be most unhappy to hear talk about whores and bastards within these hallowed walls."

I walked away from her, stiff-backed, cloaked in false piety and prudery. I hated the talk of those unchaste women who shared the King's bed…because I had decided, far too late, that Henry Plantagenet had captured my stupid, virgin heart.

Wales continued to bring grief to the crown. Rising up in equal fury to match Rhys ap Gruffudd, Dafydd Ap Owain torched Tegeingl and left it in ashes. Henry could not allow any more insurrection. Moving decisively, he gathered his army in Shropshire before marching at fastest speed to the Berwyn Mountains and the Vale of Edeyrnon beyond.

The month was August, but the burning sun that ofttimes rode the heavens in that month hid its face from my Lord. Rain lashed the earth, and the fields were slippery with mud and the rivers swollen to overflowing and dangerous to ford. Superstitious men began to desert the King's forces, saying that God turned his face away from this mission, hence the inclement weather and dangerous terrain.

Truth be told, sometimes it seemed as if the superstitions might be true. Henry's forces became stuck in a bog, the marshy ground sucking at their steeds' legs, their tents collapsing under sheets of incessant rain. Supplies were cut off by roving bands of Welshmen and disease began to decimate the English soldiers

Henry began a retreat, while his Welsh foes laughed, safe in their mountain strongholds.

An old traveller named Jessop the Tanner, journeying south to venerate the numerous relics stored in Reading Abbey was telling the nuns about Henry's unsuccessful campaign. Sister Edith had already heard the story from her messengers—she liked to keep informed—but the old pilgrim was eager to pass on his tale to the rest of us, as travellers often do.

"What happened after the retreat is a sad, sad story," Jessop murmured, shaking his tangled grey head. "I do not know if it is fit for the ears of women of the cloth."

"I was a wife for many years," sniffed one of the older nuns, Scolastica. "I came here as a widow. Even though I am professed and my duty is to serve God, I am not dead and buried yet, nor have I become some wilting little flower. Speak on."

Jessop sighed, lifting up a jug of ale to his lips. Froth clung to his beard. "The King's temper knew no bounds. They said you could hear him roaring like a lion. He took his wrath out on the hostages he had taken at Woodstock last year."

"R...revenge?" stammered Hosanna. "But they were innocent folk; they didn't cause the King's campaign to fail…"

"They were there as surety, and it was their own kind that let them down," frowned the old pilgrim, waggling a finger. "Henry was not to be made a fool of. He took the Dafydd and Conan, the sons of Owain, and Rhys' sons Maredudd, Cadwallon and Cynwrig, and many others besides…and he put out their eyes. It wasn't all he took from 'em, neither, but I won't speak of that afore women of God. Not even a brave lass like Sister Scolastica."

The nuns all gasped and made noises of dismay and disgust.

"There were girls amongst the hostages too," Jessop said sadly, knotting his bony hands together.

"Maybe we should *not* hear the rest of this tale," said Sister Concordia, a stout nun of about thirty.

"Oh they're alive, and …untouched, if that's what's worrying you, sister. Indeed, they'll likely all go to their graves untouched. Henry ordered that their noses and ears be cut off their heads so that they would be horribly disfigured for life."

Again the nuns made moaning noises of despair and revulsion.

I felt my ears grow hot and suddenly I thought I might faint. Excusing myself, I fled down the long aisle of the cloister and collapsed against a sturdy pillar at the end. Shutting my eyes, I struggled to gain control of my emotions, but in my mind, all I could see was Henry mutilating those hapless Welsh girls…then coming for me, smiling, smiling, eyes full of desire and his outstretched hands dripping with maidens' blood….

The dreams stopped.

I shut them from my mind, just as I closed the window shutters on a chill evening. I began to strike my sinful flesh if I awoke at night, following the ways of the holy sisters when desires of the flesh grew too strong to bear. I even began to think that, if he did not find a husband for me soon, I might indeed petition my Lord Father to allow me to take orders and become a postulant at the priory. In my heart, I still did not truly know if I could ever be a proper, obedient nun but locked in my cell every eve, with a crucifix and my *prie dieu*, I began to think of it with growing frequency…

As if in answer to my troubled thoughts, a messenger arrived, travelling from the west. Although he was dressed darkly, I spotted a pewter badge on his cloak that bore my father's emblem. He did not speak to me but requested an immediate audience with Prioress Edith. The request was granted and Sister Scolastica led him to Edith's receiving quarters.

Anxious, I paced the cloisters. What could he want? Were any of my kin ill…or worse? Or had father found a match for me, at long last?

Eventually, Scolastica came striding down the corridor, his robes fluttering in the wind of her speed. "Rosamund, your presence is required by the Prioress. It is urgent."

Feeling nervous and a little light-headed, I sought out the Prioress. She was sitting in her little chamber with hangings of the Virgin on the walls, holding an open parchment scroll in her hand. "Rosamund," said Lady Edith, "your father has sent two letters, one to me and one to you. He has been most kind to the nuns of Godstow for attending to your education. However, he has decided it is time for you to depart."

Reaching to the nearby table, she lifted up another scroll, sealed with blood red wax. "For you, Rosamund. Instructions from your father as to his will."

Fingers trembling and cold, I broke the wax seal and unrolled the scroll. My father's bold, slashing handwriting streaked the page. Not unsurprisingly, there were no niceties, no endearments.

The time has come for you to leave Godstow Priory. All arrangements have been made, and the Prioress has received a handsome endowment for your past care. I pray God she has made an intelligent and biddable woman of you. After Michaelmas, travelling clothes for a great lady will be sent for you to wear, and a chariot will arrive to bear you hence. I trust you will not question my decision in this matter and will be dutiful as is God's will, and follow all instructions without complaint, question or womanish fears. Do as I ask, I bid you; defy me at your peril. God go with you and remember to whom you owe duty. Your Father. W. Clifford.

I stared at the letter in silence. Prioress Edith said nothing. I supposed she knew something of my fate from her own letter but I dared not ask her. My heart was sinking. Why the secrecy, the strangeness of this missive? Father must have chosen a husband for me, as was his right, but to name no names only meant one thing—he knew I would despise the man and object to the union. My chosen husband was likely to be some dour Marcher lord, old and bloody-handed, widowed several times but wealthy and well connected. Or else he was only a boy, maybe not even ripe for the marriage bed, but of powerful bloodstock and good inheritance. I would live in his household, his legal wife and property but yet not a true wife at all, running his estate while he still played with wooden swords and my own youth diminished…

I stood up, crumpling the parchment in my hand. I would have flung it on the nearby brazier but restrained myself as such an act would have made me seem childish and petulant.

Prioress Edith glanced at me and sighed. "Do not be upset, Rosamund; I am certain Lord Clifford has only your best interests in mind, even if his intentions are presented in a rather unorthodox manner. He has been very generous to Godstow and promised to be a patron henceforth…"

"I am certain my father has many intentions indeed," I muttered, trying to keep the sarcasm from my tone. "Especially if he will benefit in some way."

Edith reddened and coughed. "Go now, child. It is nearly time for Vespers."

Grasping the mangled parchment in my cold hand, I went. Reaching my quarters, I ripped my father's letter to shreds, then wept over the pieces, watching the tear-dampened ink run in black lines over the fragments.

When I attended Vespers with the sisters, it was with swollen eyes and red runny nose. I noticed Hosanna watching me furtively, but she made no further move towards me, then or later in the night.

Still distressed, I lay down on my sleeping pallet, with the moonlight shimmering through the window-slit and the noise of the river beyond, and tried to sing to comfort my sore heart:

"Upon my right side I me lay;
Blessed Lady, to thee I pray:
For the tears that you weep
Upon your sweet son's feet,
Send me grace, for to sleep,
And good dreams for to meet,
Sleeping, waking, till morrow day shall be.
Our Lord is the fruit, Our Lady the tree,
Blessed be the blossom that sprang, Lady, of thee.
In nomine Patris et Filii et Spiritus sancti."

"Shhh!" admonished Sister Scolastica, shuffling past my cell door with a lantern swinging in her hand. "Silence is golden at this hour of the night!"

I shut my mouth with a snap and stared up at the vaulted ceiling, where a spider, large and humped, was toying with a fly trapped in its gleaming web.

Michaelmas arrived, warm and golden, and so did the dress mentioned in my father's letter. Red brocade spun with golden threads, it gleamed richly as I turned it over in my hands. Hosanna was peering over my shoulder. "That'll make a fine wedding gown," she said. "Red and gold. It will set off your hair."

I sighed. "Yes, it is a lovely gown. A pity I could not see my groom's face before gazing on the dress that I will wear for our nuptials."

"It is often that way, is it not?" asked Hosanna.

I stared at the floor. "It is. I will not complain. Complaining will do no good, will it?"

A chariot reached Godstow a few days later, trundling up the road drawn by a set of fine white horses. No device shone out from the woodwork, but it was hung inside and out with fine fabrics and had padded pillows to sit on.

Whoever my intended was, he must be rich, I thought with some slight satisfaction as I noticed a fringe of pearls on the canopy overshadowing the small windows.

The chariot was accompanied by a tall, austere man who wore crisp dark garments; again, without badge or other device. Thinking this odd, I frowned. The man noted my expression and gave a little bow. "Greetings, my Lady Clifford. Is this carriage not to your satisfaction?"

"It is a very fine carriage with handsome horses. However, I would be more restful in my mind if I knew to whom it belonged, and whom you serve."

"I am bound not to say, my Lady," he smiled ruefully. "You may call me Ranulf, though—that much I can tell you safely. But be of good cheer—all will be made clear in time. My master has words for you:

"Stetit puella
rufa tunica;
si quis eam tetigit,
tunica crepuit.
Eia!

stetit puella,

tamquam rosula;
facie splenduit,
os eius floruit.
Eia!"

I flushed but could not control a wry little smile. "A student's drinking song. I swear I heard it while in Oxford! 'A girl in a red dress that rustled, a girl who stood like a little rose'."

The man laughed. "The nuns have educated you well in Latin, Lady Rosamond."

"They have. Perhaps too well. Now let us be off. No need to put off the meeting with my intended any longer, whoever he may be."

I kissed Hosanna goodbye and said my farewells to the others. Prioress Edith emerged from her offices to watch my departure but it seemed to me she would not meet my eyes but stood staring down at her folded hands in some kind of holy contemplation.

I was past caring. My life at Godstow was over. Wearing a light and shimmering veil upon my head, my hair flowing loose down my back beneath it and the red and gold gown upon me, Ranulf handed me carefully into the chariot—a noble lady with no more pretences to the closeted life of a nun.

As I settled myself on the cushioned seat, I suddenly noticed Ranulf's cloak bell out in the wind—underneath he wore a sword. I had first thought him some kind of a coachman; however, with such a weapon he was clearly much more than that. Staring past him, I noticed that three fellows who accompanied him also bore swords beneath their long cowls, though, like Ranulf, they attempted to hide them. I suspected they were wearing mail beneath their dour workaday clothes, too.

Vaguely uneasy, but not knowing whether I should scream or make a scene, I sat back on the chariot's seat. The Prioress hobbled up to the window, sombre in her grey woollens, and made the sign of the cross over the chariot and over me. I tried to meet her eyes once again—once more, she flicked her gaze to the ground. Her expression was blank and more resigned than fearful, and I suspected she knew well what was going on.

Which was more than I knew.

Then Ranulf climbed into his seat on the chariot and flicked the reins over the backs of the fine horses, and the carriage pulled out of Godstow's courtyard and rattled away down the road beyond. Every now and then, I peeped from behind the heavy curtain masking the windows to view my surroundings. Rich green fields sped by, with church towers in the distance. I wondered how long the journey would be and how I could summon Ranulf to halt; my bladder cramped as I remembered that I had forgotten to use the privy before leaving Godstow.

Even as I pondered roadside stops with unease, the horses began to slow from a canter to a steady trot. I poked my head out the window. In the distance gleamed the turrets of a wondrous palace with a great retaining wall guarding it and miles of deep, dark forest stretching behind into a blue haze. There was only one palace in such close proximity to Oxford and that was Woodstock. The King's grandfather had built it as a hunting lodge, then filled it with unusual beasts brought from forays abroad—a camel, leopards and a porcupine. The outer wall was unusually high, not only to keep intruders out but to keep the wild creatures in; now that the land was at peace, Henry was rumoured to have kept his grandsire's tradition and imported beasts of his own for the amusement of the court.

But why would I be brought to Woodstock? My belly knotted with nerves, worsened by the juddering of the chariot. But no…wait…the chariot was rattling past the main gate with its pointed parapets and bowmen on alert, and pulling away from the main track that led to Wychwood and beyond. Curving around the side of the retaining wall, it clung to the wall's shadow and rattled downhill over bumpy ground towards the line of trees.

Soon we were deep within the woodland. Oak, ash and elder rose around us, while branches wound together to form a tight canopy. The interior of the carriage was black as midnight, and the smell of sap and leaf-mulch permeated the air. The chariot rolled to a halt, and Ranulf walked round to the carriage door, while his fellows formed a respectful guard.

Fearful and suspicious, I glared at Ranulf as I stepped from the chariot onto a bed of fallen leaves. The towering wall of the palace stood to my right; on my left was nothing but forest, miles of it running away to an unknown distance.

"Why have we stopped?" I forced a tremble from my voice. Did this man mean to dishonour me, hidden in this green fastness? Well, I would fight him tooth and nail for my honour. My hand slipped upward to touch a long, sharp pin that held my gossamer veil in place.

"I bid you tell me why you have driven me, not to the palace gate, but a clearing in the King's forest," I continued, trying to maintain an air of confidence, though I felt anything but confident.

"Lady, I am not permitted to say, but let me tell you not to fear. None in this company will bring you harm; we are sworn to protect you," Ranulf said. "Come with me." He beckoned to his men. "Hold the horses. I will not be overlong. Be silent, be discreet."

Somewhat reluctantly, I followed him across the clearing, holding up my red-gold skirts to avoid them being sullied by mud. Mushrooms crushed to nothingness underfoot; fronds batted at my face.

The wall was coming closer; I could see its great ashlar blocks through a haze of greenery. What madness was this? Did Ranulf expect to climb the wall?

My companion took a step forward and with a flourish, thrust a tangle of well-placed bushes aside to reveal a stone-lined tunnel that sank under the ground, stretching deep beneath the earth.

A secret passageway.

"My lady?" Ranulf gestured me to enter the passage.

Nervous sweat sprang out on my brow, yet what choice did I have other than to obey? If this man, this coachman who was clearly *not* an actual coachman, was lying and had evil intentions towards me, he would have them in the forest as well, and there he had his minions to assist him too.

Casting him a look that warned I would fight should he attempt to touch me, I lifted my skirts and descended into the tunnel, my feet seeking purchase on several large mossy steps that led downwards. Ferns brushed my ankles and the air smelt rank. I had gone only a few feet when I came face to face with a huge brassbound door.

"What is this?" I called over my shoulder to Ranulf. "The way is barred."

Ranulf appeared through the dimness, rummaging in a pouch fastened to his belt. "Just a moment, Lady Rosamund. The key…I have a key."

From the leather bag, he pulled out a large iron key, gleaming dully in the half-light. He held it up; his teeth flashed in the gloom as he grinned. "This key is also key to my life, Lady Rosamund."

"I do not understand." I frowned.

"Should I lose it or let it fall into the hands of those not authorised to use it…my life would be forfeit."

I wanted to ask more but suspected no answer would be forthcoming. Next to me, Ranulf was opening the door to reveal another length of tunnel. It was black inside, dark as a dragon's maw. At the end, the corridor split into a fork, with two long arms branching out from it.

Taking a deep breath, I stepped inside and the door was closed—and locked—behind me.

My guide Ranulf ushered me on to the fork in the passageway. "To the left, my Lady," he murmured and, mercifully, after a few more feet stumbling through the fuggy darkness, we reached a staircase that veered upwards. Ascending the steps, we reached a wooden hatch that my erstwhile companion thrust aside with an effort.

I burst out into the light, cold air striking my face.

And I screamed.

A shadow was stretching over me, a strange Green Man, a Woodwose with a spiky, briar-strewn mane fanning out around his head. His arms shook and shuddered, reaching…and then I realised the truth. My assailant was not real. The 'Woodwose' was merely a bush, artfully cut by talented gardeners into a man's form. The 'arms' that had reached for me were but branches, swaying in the wind.

I gazed beyond the verdant figure. There were more such artworks, guarding a paved path that led into what appeared to be some sort of garden. A horse head, a tower, a knight, an axe; other shapes beyond them. They rustled and moved as the wind caressed their leafy frames. Between each one stood statuary, lewd figures of pagan gods and goddesses, their bodies entwined in frantic lovemaking. Behind these were sheets of deadly looking thorns, twisted round wooden frames, which stopped one from peering into the heart of the garden…or getting through without being hooked and torn on the spikes.

"What is this awful place?" I breathed, rounding on Ranulf with fists clenched. "It…it is like a sorcerer's garden!"

"It is known as the Bower," he said. "Come, Lady, we must not tarry here. You will come to know this place…eventually. But now I must show you to the Tower, where you will stay." He gestured across the grotesque garden to a tall, pointed grey tower with a conical turret wrought of dark red slate. It looked fierce, like some wild animal's fang piercing the sky.

"And we must pass through this…Bower to get there?" I stared with fear and distaste at the statue of a satyr mounting a goat, and at another where a flapping swan was ravishing a nymph.

He nodded. "Aye, and I must ask that you stay close behind me and do not speak, for the way through is not a simple thing and I must think clearly. If I have not remembered what I was entrusted to learn, we could be wandering here for hours."

He went down the path into the garth and I followed him, averting my gaze from the topiary and the obscene statues. It seemed we went round and round for ages, twisting here and there as the pathway snaked, reaching dead ends where bristling hedges sprang, then slipping through unexpected gaps carved in the shrubbery.

Finally, though, the serpentine path ended and a wide, oak door became visible. One more topiary figure loomed, and once again I cringed in fright…it was the Green Lady, she who had guarded Clifford Castle—the sacrificed maiden. She leant against the fabric of the Tower, arms stretched toward the light, breasts dangling with red berries, ivy shoots springing from her hands and embracing the stonework.

"I…I cannot…" I gasped, gazing up into the blank green face. The face of change, the face of fate.

Ranulf stared at me as if I had lost my wits and used his key to unlock the door. Hurriedly he pulled me out of the dreadful Bower…into a small vestibule where a staircase spiralled up through the body of the Tower. Yet another closed door stood to one side; from under it drifted the mouth-watering scent of freshly baked bread.

I glanced at my companion. "I will show you," he said, "since you will be mistress here."

Using his key, he unlocked this new door. We stepped into a brightly lit kitchen. What a difference! The kitchen was homely, ordinary. A brace of rabbits lay on a long table, alongside a pheasant, half-plucked. A burly cook in a white apron was poking a potboy, who was scouring a vast vat. Other servants moved about, busy with their chores.

As Ranulf and I appeared, clattering onto the flagstones, all the servants glanced up with startled faces, then, unexpectedly, began to bow or curtsey with eyes downcast. It was as if I were royalty! Due to my birth, I was used to some deference by the servant class but never to this extreme.

Leaving the kitchen, we re-entered the vestibule. Ranulf gestured to the stairs I had noted earlier. I began to climb, heading upwards toward an unknown destination.

Torches burned in brackets on the walls, but the place seemed almost...empty, dead—my footsteps echoed. Such a stronghold should be teeming with life, with members of the household, with servants going about their daily business, with hounds and the lord's children, with minstrels singing and playing.

Instead, it was silent. Eerie. Yet, instinctively I knew that it was occupied.

Another door loomed, bound with brass bands polished to a high sheen. Ranulf opened it and waved me through onto what was the first floor. I stood motionless for a moment until my companion gestured that I might wander at leisure. "Please look, my Lady, I beg you."

Moving forward, I noticed a hall, richly decorated but silent as the grave, with empty musicians' gallery and attached to it, a tiny but ornate chapel with painted glass windows and golden candlesticks upon the altar. A small solar was tucked in the back, and here I finally saw some human faces—several ladies who dropped low curtseys before vanishing down a corridor to what I supposed were their quarters.

"Who are they?" I asked.

"Your ladies in waiting. They are here to serve you," said Ranulf, "as are the cooks and servants on the ground level. These women, carefully chosen for discretion and constancy, will see to your personal needs such as tending to your wardrobe and drawing the bath. I am sure they will eventually become your friends."

"That is rather presumptuous, Ranulf," I said, with a sense of unease. The locked doors, the empty spaces, the women with bowed heads and scurrying feet...It felt wrong.

Ranulf made no answer. Having shown me the hall, chapel and the women who were to be my companions, he was retreating from this middle level toward the spiral staircase, which continued up another story. Proceeding up the stairs, he gestured me on for the last leg of our strange journey.

Soon a final door loomed, its panels covered in a sheet of beaten copper, which bore an image of the Virgin and Child; the key rattled into the lock one last time and it glided open.

This time, Ranulf did not go into the chamber beyond but stood courteously aside. "Your personal apartments, Lady Rosamund. I will not enter here for it is not appropriate for me to do so. Please inspect them at your leisure."

Wondering, I pushed past him and strode into a bedchamber with a high sharply-angled ceiling; it was clearly at the top of the conical tower. Secular scenes were painted on the walls—winter embodied as a frosty-faced maiden; summer as a ripe-breasted nymph with roses bound in her hair. There were huge, hanging tapestries of great worth—scenes of hounds and horses bounding through woodland and delicate unicorns with swivelled horns—and near the arched window, a massive bed with an oaken frame hung in gold. A King's bed...and sure enough, embroidered on the lavish quilt, were the golden lions that Henry Plantagenet favoured.

"It is he who has summoned me here..." I breathed, and then, over my shoulder to Ranulf, I cried, almost hysterical, "It's the King, isn't it? It's the King who has ordered me here!"

Ranulf recoiled, seemingly shocked by the fury in my voice. And yes, I *was* furious. Oh yes, I had spent uncounted nights thinking of our brief encounter, of how we would never meet again, of how my father would see me respectably wed and how my embraces with England's King would fade into the mists of memory...and now *THIS*. I had been brought here like a possession, a slave, with my own father's connivance, and maybe, it seemed, that of the Prioress of Godstow. A *nun*, by Christ's Nails—a woman sworn to chastity agreed to see me bundled off to concubinage.

"Answer me!" I rounded on the stunned Ranulf. "It's all on his orders, isn't it? Am I a prisoner here?"

"A prisoner? No, of course not!" said Ranulf shakily, taking a step backwards. "You have done no wrong."

"Then can I leave unimpeded?" Threateningly, I stepped towards the door.

Alarm flooded his face. "No, Lady Rosamund, I beg you, do not make this situation any more difficult than it already is."

"So I *am* a prisoner..." The fight went out of me and my legs turned to jelly. I slumped onto the edge of the bed, shoulders drooping, and at that moment Ranulf slipped out of the chamber without a single word. With sinking heart, I heard the key, his precious key, click noisily in the lock. Then his footsteps faded into the distance, faint echoes in that large, near-empty tower.

I sat in shock for a while amidst the opulence, the beautiful tapestries, the soft imported rugs, the chests that were doubtless full of fripperies for me. Then I rose shakily and went to the high arched window, flinging open the gilt shutter with a bang.

Far in the distance, the turrets of Woodstock palace were swathed in a twilight mist. Hundreds of feet below me, circled by a second great wall without gate or breach, was the twisted, obscene garden I had walked through—which I now realised was *not* simply a maze wrought of interwoven thorn-bushes and sculptured trees, as I had first thought.

Instead, it was a labyrinth, like that of the Minotaur in the tales of the old Greeks.

The haunts of the Bull who was also a Man, fierce and terrible. I returned to the bed, my hands trembling, to wait for him.

He came two days later, but not as a beast tramping up the stairs, charging forward with the fury of his lusts driving him onwards. He came quietly, his boots making a soft, determined tread, the sound of the key rattling in the lock both inherently exciting and yet ominous.

Dressed in a plain brown tunic and rain-stained cloak—Henry cared not for fine garments since he spent so much time in the saddle—he came to me straight from the hunt or from hawking. His deep reddish hair was cropped slightly shorter than I remembered, a style closer to that of the old Norman lords than to modern young men, who wore their hair longer and curled at the nape of the neck, and his eyes were as stormy and determined as ever, flecked with wolfish amber lights.

A long shuddering sigh escaped my lips.

"My Lady Rosamund." Legs apart, he halted, the rain dripping from his thrown back hood, looking me up and down.

"Your Grace!" I sank to my knees.

"Rise! Rise!" His strong, calloused hand went to mine, assisting me to my feet; then he lifted the other hand to my face, stroking my cheek with a gloved finger.

"You are more beautiful, Rosamund Clifford, than ever I remember."

"Beautiful enough to imprison?" The words burst out; I did not know where such impertinence came from. He was the King. He could do what he wished with any lowly subject.

He stared in surprise for a moment, and then said, "Is that how you see it?"

"Your Grace…" My troubled thoughts flooded out now. "I am behind locked doors. Men who would not reveal their full names brought me here. My father sent me a mysterious letter, telling me I must question naught and obey completely. What else can I think?"

"Perhaps are here for your safety," he said softly.

"What do you mean?" I had not thought of such a scenario. "Who would harm me?"

Henry looked thoughtful and his eyes narrowed. "The Queen can be a jealous woman and her reach is long."

I blushed and bowed my head. "At the moment," I swallowed, "I am just Rosamund, a maiden fresh from the convent at Godstow. The Queen...at this time... has no need to be jealous of me."

Henry reached out, catching a strand of my hair and coiling it about his forearm. Then he let it drop. "When first we met at Clifford castle, you entranced me as no women before. I cannot say why, for I will be truthful—I have lain with women unnumbered, from whores to widows to other men's wives. I mostly avoided virgins, I must admit—too much trouble!—and despite my desire for your body, I restrained myself in the face of your fear and innocence. You have matured—I can see it in your face—but still, I am no monster." He stepped aside, gestured at the door with the flickering torches beyond. "You may leave, if it is your will."

The rebel in me wanted to cry that I was not an animal to be bartered by my ambitious sire or bought by a King, but I bit down hard on my lip, as I knew such a move would be foolish. Angry as I was by the deception, the secrecy...I could not deny how often I had thought of Henry, remembering his muscular arms, the strength of his naked torso, heavy with muscle and covered with the scars of warfare. Something...*bound* us, although I did not know why or what it was. I did *not* want to leave him, although I feared and resented being here,

"It is *not* my will to leave." I took a deep breath. "Although it is also not my wish to be a concubine instead of a wife. Even to a mighty King." I began to shake, fearing that I had indeed gone too far. "There...I have said it. Punish me if it is *your* will, my Lord King."

I expected him to be angry. Instead, after a few seconds of silence, he flung back his head and roared with laughter.

"Is that what it is? The nuns instilled good morals in you, did they?"

"I have always had them."

"It is not your morals I remember, Lady." His eyes slipped from my face to my breast.

I was sure my cheeks were the colour of fire.

Suddenly Henry reached out and grasped my hand. "If a vow is what is bothering you, I can make it right...Come with me, come with me!"

Slamming the door, he directed me not to the bedchamber but to the private chapel attached to it, with its white marble altar and paintings of mournful-eyed saints. The Rood shone gold behind the small, ornate screen. There was no priest, just us two…and God, who saw all.

"Your Grace, what are you doing?" I gasped, as he pulled me in front of the altar.

"God!" he cried out, his voice jovial (and, I thought, unseemly). "Before you, maker of all, ruler of rulers, I Henry Plantagenet do utter my intent—one day I shall have Rosamund Clifford to be my bride. I do swear that we shall be as husband and wife."

I was horrified, my mouth hanging open, aghast. "My…my lord King, but you are already married!"

"Aye," he said, "but she is older than me, much older. I will surely outlive her. She can be wicked and wilful too, Rosamund; she has already had one marriage annulled. Albeit to marry me! She may well go for another annulment if provoked. I fear I'd have to fight her for Aquitaine, though—one of the main reasons I married her. That and the fact she was like riding a wild horse in bed."

"My Lord King." I hung my head. "It is not my position to chide—but you should not make such jests or speak with such frankness in God's chapel."

"I do not jest," he said. "It is my intent. One day, God willing. So…we are as good as married. Do not fret about it any longer."

The King led me back to the bedchamber. My head reeled; I was stunned by his behaviour… To make such a promise would be considered binding in other circumstances, but this was complete madness. He was already married, which surely invalidated any promises made to me...but many Kings and nobles wriggled out of unwanted marriages. A sudden case of previously unknown consanguinity usually worked or declarations of barrenness (certainly not applicable to fertile Eleanor!) or impotence on the part of the husband (clearly not Henry's problem either!)

Blithe and unperturbed, Henry rang the bell by the door that summoned the servants in the levels below. "I will have wine brought and sweetmeats and other delicacies. A pheasant from the park maybe? Have you eaten well since you arrived at Woodstock, Rosamund? Have my servants been looking after you?"

I nodded. "Yes, the ladies who also dwell in this tower have been most attentive. Even though they always come together…they seem to think I might try to overpower them and run away."

He laughed. "I still half fear you might….but you won't, will you?"

I shook my head.

"Kiss me, Rosamund." He fell into a chair and drew me onto his lap, his mouth seeking mine, his hands lifting the soft, curling river of my hair. "I have dreamed of this while in the arms of so many others," he groaned.

Footsteps sounded outside, then a sharp knock on the door. Henry made a disgusted noise. "I almost wished I hadn't called them. My appetite is now for…other things."

Nonetheless, he allowed the servants entry; in silence, with downcast eyes, they placed their gilt trays on the table, bowed and left.

In silence, we both ate and drank. The strong, rich wine calmed my fluttering nerves somewhat.

Suddenly Henry, taking one final gulp of wine, cast down his goblet. "Enough. My thirst has been slaked…for wine."

"Mine too, my lord King." My voice was feeble.

"The dress…you are wearing the dress I sent."

"Aye, my lord King."

"Call me Henry…it is what I wish. You look fair in the dress…"

"My thanks, my lor…Henry."

"…but, take it off."

Shaking, my hands went to the fastenings of my dress; normally I would have expected my ladies to help me disrobe but they were down below, tucked into their own apartments. I doubted Henry would wait for them to attend me. Clumsily, I shrugged my way out of the dress and stood in my chemise, feeling as foolish as embarrassed.

Henry was appreciative, however. "Now, the rest. No…wait…let me do it." Rising from his seat, he looped an arm around my waist and pushed me onto the bed. With practised fingers, he began to unlace the ties at the front of my chemise.

I could hear his breathing deepen, as he pulled the cloth away from my breasts, baring them to his sight, his touch. "Those who praise Eleanor's beauty have never gazed upon the beauties of the Rose of the World," he said, running his thumbs over my body, teasing, exciting. "Rosebuds which will blossom only to my touch."

He pressed me down on the bed, his lips following where his fingers had caressed. Heat ran through me, despite the fact the fire had died in the brazier. If I was sinning, I now knew why people committed this sin; why chastity was so hard to keep, why the nuns, monks, and priests thundered about the lure of carnal temptations.

I was completely nude now, the chemise discarded, and Henry was exploring my flesh from head to toe, nuzzling the hollow of my neck, kissing and licking breasts and belly, caressing the growing warmth between my thighs. He had cast off his own garments and once again, I saw his terrible battle scars, his chest and arms rippling with muscles honed by the use of the sword. But now I saw more too—the root of him.

He heard my indrawn breath, saw where my gaze went. "Are you impressed, my love? Am I not like the mighty bull?"

Impressed? More frightened than anything…but I would not tell him that in case he was angered. He might be my lover but he was also the King, and Kings are often fickle and vain.

"Very impressed…Henry, you are magnificent," I whispered, and as before, I thought of him as the Bull-man, the Minotaur, master of the labyrinth beyond the Tower walls.

He clutched me to him, lifting my hips, not as gentle as he might have been, all pretty words fled in his need. The Bull roared and I cried out in answer, in pain…and then, to my surprise, in unexpected pleasure.

Henry woke me early the next day and rolled me onto my back, kissing and caressing, savouring my flesh with lips and tongue. I was stiff and sore after the previous night but the discomfort as he claimed my body was less great than it had been at first…and the pleasure far greater.

"You learn fast," he said when he had finished, leaning on his elbow and gazing down at me, toying with the sweat soaked strand of red hair that coiled around the mound of my breast. "Sometimes those who have been maids overlong and schooled by nuns become cold or unduly fearful! That is one reason why, till now, I have enjoyed mainly widows and harlots."

"I aim to please you, Henry," I said. "I always will."

"And you do, you do." He suddenly pushed me from the bed, playfully slapping my bottom. "But we must not be slugabeds, lying here all day like hounds in the sun. I will take you in the gardens, and we will walk together. Would you like that?"

"I would," I nodded. I was no so sure about the garden, but I would not spoil the pleasure of the moment.

So Henry summoned the servants, and they brought him a great tub and bathed him under a canopy, and the girls chosen as my maids emerged from their quarters to lave my skin with sweet rosewater, then dress me in another fine gown from one of the chests in my apartments. They kept their heads down, made no eye contact, did not chatter as did the ladies back in my parents' castle. For all my initial harsh words about presumption to Henry's servant Ranulf, I hoped one day that this distance between the women and me would diminish, and that I would be seen as more than the King's concubine.

Once we were cleansed and dressed suitably, sops were brought to us in bowls, and an old priest from some local village brought in to say Mass. He was dithery and half-blind, and seemed very embarrassed to be there.

"Father Morland," Henry said, with a grin. Evidently, he knew the old man from long ago. "Come, look not so dismayed. Say Mass, and then hear our confessions! You know what they will be!"

"Your Grace," said the priest in his high, tremulous voice. "I do say you speak inappropriately…as ever…"

"Father, do not vex me!" Henry rolled his eyes. "We have known each other since I first came to England, and I thought you understood me well. I beg you do not become troublesome like my old friend Thomas Becket."

"I am always loyal, your Grace," admonished Father Morland, waving an admonishing finger at the King. "But I have a care for your mortal soul…and for that of the, er, ah…" His rheumy gaze landed on me; he squinted, eyes crinkling up as he tried to focus, "…this young woman."

"Then get on with it, man!" bawled Henry, taking my hand. "And you may as well know the 'young woman's' name. It is Rosamund Clifford. And, just so you know, she is not a whore, harlot, bawd, trull, or slattern. We may live in what you consider 'sin'…but that may change one day. Yes, one day who knows what Rosamund Clifford might be?"

The little priest's head bobbed on its long, gaunt neck. "Whatever you say, your Grace. I only minister to souls. Whatever you do or plan is between you and God. Just, I bid you, think carefully. England has already been through civil war after Stephen's usurpation. We are now at peace. We want it to remain so, and pray our Lord King does too."

"Do you think there would be fighting over the Lady Rosamund?" Henry said with a wry smile.

"Stranger things have happened," said Father de Morland. "Was not Troy ruined over a woman and many great warriors slain? Remember, my lord King; the Queen is a powerful and headstrong woman, unlike most other women. That you realise this, you cannot deny, for if she were not, you would not have built this tower here for your…paramour."

Henry's face turned crimson now; his good humour fading rapidly. "Father Morland, I have been patient enough. The only sermons I want to hear are those to do with the Bible! Stop lecturing me, man, and let us hear the word of the Lord!"

That startled the old priest. Whatever doubts he had about Queen Eleanor or me, he spoke them not again.

When Mass was over and Father Morland had been guided from the Tower through the servants' tunnel and away to whatever village he came from, Henry guided me down from the turret, to the middle floor and then into the vestibule on the first floor. Several servants passed us on the stairs; they fell to the ground like fallen gaming pieces at the sight of us, grovelling.

Hand clasping mine, Henry led me outside into the garden labyrinth he had designed. I savoured its strangeness more slowly this time, my fear gradually receding. With a new sense of wonder, I examined the bushes cut into their fantastical shapes. They were like subtleties at a feast, designed by some gardener's craft, but whereas at a feast the shaped puddings were clever and brought delight to the beholder—these tree sculptures seemed sinister, ominous. Besides the ones I had already seen when I arrived, there was a green lion raising a shaggy head and a leafy dog baring twig-fangs whittled into spikes. A rounded head with troll-like nose pushed out of a stone grotto, mouth gaping as if eager to consume me in its verdant heart.

I crouched closer to Henry at the sight of this last one, my unease returning, but he did not notice as he continued to talk about the skills of those he had commissioned to build this woodland bower. "Nothing has ever been seen in England quite like this," he said with pride. "I based it on Italian gardens, but with a twist of my own. And it is for you, all for you."

Turning a corner, we reached the heart of the labyrinth. A well stood before us, dark water bubbling and churning out from an unseen source. It reminded me of a saint's shrine, with a newly built cover of fine Caen stone and carven heads set in niches on either side on the entranceway. The carvings were not of saints, though—the one on the left was a maiden, the other a crowned king.

"Rosamund's Well," said Henry. "It used to be known as Everswell but no more. It will be named for you forever after, and long after we are gone pilgrims will come to this place and say, 'Drink here, all those who love and love well, in memory of those who loved before ye'."

I gazed down into the well water in silence. Love. If Henry foresaw a future where our union was remembered with affection, *I* saw the waters muddied, the well cover collapsed into the pool, the Tower behind me shattered with bats soaring from its ruins. He was my lord and now he was my lover, but even in my innocent youth, I was aware that men often spoke of 'love' differently to women. Did I truly believe, for all his sweet words, in the night and on this fair day that he would be with me forever, no matter what? That he would remain true to me, in mind if not body despite his reputation?

"Why so sad?" he asked, noticing my pensive expression.

"My lord…Henry…it is only because I know you soon will be gone from here." That was true too.

He sighed. "Yes. My clever Rosamund. I am King, and I have duties to attend. Tomorrow I must be on my way by dawn's breaking. I shall take ship to Brittany—I plan to make my son Geoffrey Duke there when the old Duke dies. He will marry young Constance, the Duke's heiress."

I glanced over my shoulder at the Tower. The sun was moving round it; a shadow stretched over us like a warning finger. "Take me with you. I fear to be here alone for months."

"I cannot…it would not be safe, as I have said." There was a hint of steel, of impatience, in his voice. "You will not be alone. I have supplied you with ladies and servants, and the old priest will come each day to minister to your spiritual needs."

"But will I be locked up in the top of the tower? " My voice trembled, despite myself. "As I have been since I arrived here?"

He sighed, folding his arms. "No…no…I suppose that *would* seem like imprisonment. I do not intend for you to abide here in distress. I will leave instructions that you are to be permitted, even in my absence, to have full access to the second level—to the hall, solar and public chapel, and to the gardens. Once a week, I will send my personal musicians for your entertainment. I forbid you to tarry in the kitchen, however, other than to give orders to Cook, or seek the two passages that lead to the outside world. You are not to allow any unauthorised soul within the Tower, even if they offer sweet blandishments or claim they are messengers from your family. Your ladies are not to be permitted to enter the labyrinth—only you may access it, along with the gardeners that I will send when needed. All folk must exit through the kitchens be they of great or low estate. Do you understand? Do you swear to abide by my rules?"

"I swear it." A small concession, at least!

"And if anything seems amiss, if strangers break into the Tower or you hear that violent men are gathered without its walls, promise me you will fly into the topmost chamber and bar the door from within. Swear to me that you will do that, too."

"I hardly imagine this is a great worry, with so many locked doors to pass through already."

"Swear it!" he barked, his voice rolling like thunder over the labyrinth.

I swore.

Then he smiled with surprising softness for a man so powerful and war-like, pressed my hand to his lips like a polished courtier, and led me back towards the gaunt grey stalk of the Tower.

True to his word, he left for Brittany the next day.

Gifts came by the week. A lute to play, the finest material for my embroidery, shoes from Paris, gowns wrought of cloth of gold. A little tri-coloured dog called Patch. Rubies and emeralds set in gold. Pearled headdresses.

Henry made certain I knew he did not forget me...but I wished sorely that he could be with here instead of across the sea.

A loved and cosseted mistress I might have been, but the time we spent together was scarce indeed.

I grew to know the ladies hired to attend upon me; there were three, Juliana, Blanche, and Orable. It was hard to form a rapport, though; they were always circumspect and of sombre demeanour, though they performed their tasks well enough. Sometimes, if prompted, I could get news of the outside world from Blanche, who seemed the most affable of the three. Likewise, I garnered news from the old priest, Father Morland, who came daily to the Tower and was not nearly so prim and condemnatory as he seemed at first.

"I have been to Godstow," he said to me one day after he had celebrated Mass. "The Prioress sends you greetings...and Sister Hosanna too."

"Do they?" I was holding my dog Patch in my arms, wriggling and licking my chin. "I miss them," I said thoughtfully.

Father Morland drew closer, his eyes kindly. "Child...yes, you are not much more than a child, are you? I tell you, Lady Rosamund, Prioress Edith would have you back at Godstow. You could repent of your ungodly life here and live a truly good life with the sisters."

"What would the King say?" I said

"He could surely not argue with a calling to the church! It is not as if...as if you are his wife."

I hid my face in Patch's fur. Father Morland did not know that Henry had called me 'wife' before the altar, although he had certainly dropped hints of future plans within the churchman's presence. Even if there was never an annulment, Queen Eleanor *was* an old woman, over forty! She would not live forever...

"I could help you to go there..."

"No, no, I could not put you in any danger, Father," I said hastily. I had no wish to go anywhere on a permanent basis, as pleasant as it would be to see Hosanna and the others. Not if it meant giving up my royal lover. My reluctance towards him was gone; the die was cast. It was as if our union had been fated—like the doom of the tragic Green Lady who hugged Clifford's Castle with her dead, verdant arms.

Father Morland patted my arm as though I were a small child. "Your care for my wellbeing is very kind, Lady Rosamund. Just do not forget, Prioress Edith would hold the door of Godstow open to you. If you ever need sanctuary, it is there."

For some reason, a chill went through me at his words, even though they were meant to be comforting and compassionate. Patch must have sensed the change in my mood, for he lowered his head and uttered a soft little growl.

"I will remember, Father," I said to the aged priest. "I promise."

Winter arrived, bringing days of black skies and heavy snow. Outside the Tower the world was white; below, in the Bower, Rosamund's Well was frozen and the clipped heads of the bushes topped with domes of white.

I sat in the hall, reclining in a window embrasure and staring out while snowflakes swirled down from the heavens. I wondered where Henry slept that night. He was constantly busy and often away in his lands in Aquitaine and Anjou. That frightened me more than I cared to admit. What if he should never return, what if a fever should take him or an assassin strike? There had been more trouble earlier this year with his old friend Becket. The Archbishop had excommunicated the King's chief Justiciar and other highborn magnates and counsellors. Becket used excommunication as a weapon and Henry was reported to be highly displeased by his actions. Again. Important meetings had also kept the King busy at Clarendon, the royal Plantagenet palace situated between Salisbury and Winchester, where the Dermot Mc Murrough, King of Leinster, begged for aid against a host of warring Irish petty Kings, each one eager for territory. Henry's eye had been on Ireland since before he took the throne, and he had sent one of his most stalwart allies, Richard de Clare, to deal with Mc Murrough's problem.

If the King was overworked and much vexed by the year's events, I was not in the happiest of moods myself. It was Christmas Eve. Servants had decorated the Tower with holly and ivy from the nearby woods and the cooks in the kitchen had received suckling piglets, capons, geese and even a swan by the King's decree.

But there was not truly going to be a Christmas feast on the morrow, not with me sitting alone at the head of the hall, with only my demure, downcast ladies in attendance—unless one counted the gaggle of musicians and acrobats Henry had promised to send for my pleasure. Even in my father's castle, old and small though it was, Christmas had been a time of great celebration, with all the local lords of the Border gathered round and much merriment and gift giving. The villagers would skate on the river and kindle a huge Christmas bonfire, while the three daughters of fierce Clifford would go amongst the revellers, sliding precariously across the snowy cobbles in our best gowns to hand out coins to the poor and infirm.

I wished I could walk freely outside the Bower walls and visit all the little villages beyond to bring them cheer, just as I had done as a girl in Herefordshire...but it was forbidden. The doors leading to the tunnels and the outside world were barred to me. For my safety, according to Henry.

I thought of the woman I was supposed to be kept safe from, the Queen whom I had neither met nor seen. The beautiful, intelligent but impure Queen who was growing aged, though 'twas said, still retained unsurpassed beauty. Even if Eleanor's morals were questionable, she had done her duty by Henry, giving him a gaggle of children, William, who had died young, then Henry, Matilda, Richard, Geoffrey, Leonora and Joan.

What had I given him? My maidenhood and my love. An oath to stay here, trapped in a Tower like some mythical princess in a tale of old...That was all. I would not be able to give him children in the manner Eleanor had, unless he managed to visit me more often; though I had to admit, when my courses arrived after he first departed for Brittany, a flush of relief surfed through me. It was too soon in our union, we were still, in truth, not much more than strangers, albeit intimate ones, and the thoughts of being locked in the Tower alone with a babe, even a royal bastard, were not particularly pleasant ones....

"I want to retire for the night," I said petulantly to my maid Juliana. "I want to be alone to pray." It was still Advent, until tomorrow—as good an excuse as any to hide away in self-indulgent misery.

"As you wish, Madam." Juliana curtseyed; as usual, she did not raise her eyes to meet mine. No hint of either approval or disapproval there. She was the least animated of my maids, the one hardest to read. "I will attend you."

Together we approached the narrow stairs to my apartments, lit by a flow of torches and tapers, their wobbling light casting weird shadows across the walls. Blanche and Orable said nothing, as was their wont, and continued working in silence on their embroidery frames.

Patch bounded on before me and curled himself in ball on the rug in my chamber. Juliana helped me remove my outer gown and brushed down my chemise—a new one sent to me by the King that was fashioned from fine lace and decorated with gold thread, tassels and roundels. Then she dutifully brushed my long hair, her strokes firm then growing a little rougher, almost a punishment that pulled strands straight from my scalp. Furtively I glanced at her expression from behind a hank of curling hair and was dismayed to see that she wore a satisfied little smirk. She was enjoying hurting me.

I would not have it. "Stop!" I ordered. She was older than I was but I did not care. I was a lord's daughter and the King's leman.

She stopped but held the brush raised in her hand almost as if she planned to use it as a weapon. When and why had she taken against me so? I had done nothing to her—had even tried striking up friendship at first, which was hastily rebuffed.

I had to put an end to this insolence —if that is what it was. As the daughter of Clifford, I had to assert my authority. I knew if I showed any weakness my position here would be precarious in the extreme.

"You are too rough," I said curtly. "No more. The fire is nearly out too. Stoke it." I pointed to the dully glow in the iron brazier.

Juliana flung down the hairbrush, walked over to the brazier in silence and lumped a handful wood into it. She began jabbing at it with a poker, her motions showing clear annoyance.

"You are dismissed now." I turned my back on her, listening as her footsteps vanished down the stairs.

Glad that she was gone, I closed the door. Even though the fire leapt up now, a cold shudder passed through me.

Dreamlessly I slept, wrapped in the coverlet. Outside the winter storm raged, winds shrieking, snow hissing as it battered the wooden shutters.

Suddenly I stirred, moved uneasily. A distant bang. A draught of cold air. Lying near the guttered fire, Patch gave a small warning growl.

Bleary-eyed I gazed towards the door. I hadn't locked it. Should I have? Now I could hear someone approaching—mounting the stairs, running up them two at a time.

Too fast! Something was wrong! My heart began to hammer and Patch leapt to his feet and began to bark furiously, the fur on his hackles raised.

The door burst open, hitting the wall with a resounding bang. A big, bear- like shape burst in, blocking out the light of the half-dead torches in the stairwell.

I screamed. Patch's barking grew furious.

"God's Teeth, woman, call off your dog!" A familiar voice boomed out.

It was the King.

I reached for Patch, grabbing him by the scruff of the neck and commanding his silence. His loud howls vanished as he saw Henry and he began to wag his tail furiously.

"Your Grace…I was not expecting you." I crawled out of bed and curtseyed.

"That is clear by your attire…but here I am. Will you give me no better welcome, Rosamund?"

Hastily I put Patch into my personal privy, masked by decorative hangings in an alcove where the turret jutted out beyond the encircling wall, and shut the door on his bristling snout. I could hear him digging at the doorstep with his paws; he was not happy about his confinement but he would have to stay.

As I dropped the hangings into place and turned around, Henry was standing behind me, grinning. Melting snowflakes dripped from his brows and hair. He enfolded me in his arms; he smelt of leather, horses, winter…and drink.

He had been feasting…Early, as it was still Advent and the Church forbade all good men and women to feast until Christmas Day dawned. But when did Henry listen overmuch to priests?

"Henry…my lord," I placed my finger against his lips even as he tried to place a wobbly kiss on my mouth.

"What is it?" He looked cross. "Why are you so reticent? Have you tired of me already? Are you fickle and untrue?"

"Of course not!" I cried, shocked that he should suggest that I was an inconstant woman. "But it is Christmas Eve…and…not only did I not expect your presence, I did not expect you…you to have imbibed so much wine!" As the words exited my mouth, I feared I might sound shrewish and finished lamely, "You might have been in danger riding about the countryside drunk in a snow storm."

Henry flung back his head and laughed in that booming, careless way of his. Propriety meant little to the Plantagenet. "You think I am drunk, little Rosamund?" He pulled me closer, hands on my hips. "I am merely celebrating. Celebrating. A child was born today!"

"What child?" I mumbled, confused, not sure if he was talking about Our Lord or some other.

"In Beaumont Palace in Oxford, a boy was born today…my son. Black haired and howling like a demon from the moment he entered the world. I swear he attacked the wet nurse's teat with more gusto than any babe I have ever seen—he will be a lady's man, will my newest son. I have decided that he be called John, for in a few days it will be the Feast of St John the Evangelist."

A son! I did not quite know how to answer. I had not even known the Queen was enceinte; it was unusual for a woman her age to still bear fruit.…

"You look strange, Rosamund…so thoughtful. What is the matter?" Henry was quieter now. Reaching to his belt-pouch, he brought forth a brooch decorated with pearls and sapphires. "My Christmas gift for you. Do you like it?"

"It is beautiful," I said, taking it. It was, but all I could think of was Henry at Beaumont Palace with Eleanor…with their new babe. "Alas, I have nothing of value to give you in return."

"Oh, yes, you do, my fair beloved." His lips trailed along my throat, finding the pulse, fastening to its beat. "Come, Rosamund, let us waste no more time and go to bed. I have missed you more than I can say."

It was a sin to have carnal relations on this holy night, but we were sinners anyway and I dared not gainsay him.

He lifted me up and deposited me on the bed, his strong firm hands pulling my garments from me, experienced and bold. There was no more talk of the new baby, little John Plantagenet, but as I lay there, with my lord King, my lover's hot, hard body thrusting upon mine, all I could think of was that nine months back he had lain likewise with Eleanor. *Eleanor*, who in my foolish imagination I had begun to see as a crone, a shrewish harridan whose desirability and fertility was fading rapidly. But it was clearly not true. And for all Henry had talked of a future for us, she was still Queen and still producing his legitimate children.

I, on the other hand, was cloistered away from the world near Woodstock, unknown to all but the King's closest confidants. Henry would admire me for a while, stroke and cosset me like a beautiful pearl in a shell...and then the shell would snap shut and I would be jealously hidden away again.

The old unease consumed me—I felt not so much 'beloved' as a prisoner. Henry's pretty possession.

As Henry heaved off me, rolled to one side of the bed and began to snore, drink and the aftermath of passion getting the better of him, I began to weep quietly, unnoticed.

Outside the Tower, the snow continued to fall.

I had come to a new agreement with Henry. He was not pleased but he had cleaved to me in my wishes.

I would now have some freedom *beyond* Tower and Bower.

"Rumours spread," I told him, "and Queens have spies. If Eleanor does not know about me by now, she must be either blinkered or addle-pated and I doubt that very much from all you have told me. Henry…you must allow me out of here."

"You wish to leave me?" The hint of trepidation in his voice pleased me. He truly feared to lose my love.

"No. And I am happy to dwell here, but not for years on end. Not isolated. I want your permission to visit the nuns at Godstow…and Oxford when the Queen is not at Beaumont Palace. I promise I will not draw undue attention to myself."

"I am not happy about this plan." Henry's eyes narrowed. "You might be followed back by agents of Eleanor."

"Then have more guards set upon the door. Make the Tower more of a castle…less of a prison."

His eyes were brooding but I could see that he was mulling over my words. "I do understand your concerns. Well, if it would make you happy…"

"Nothing would make me happier, other than for you to dwell here with me day in and day out. Or for me to dwell with you…elsewhere."

It was the first time I had dared mention living with him as man and wife in the world beyond the walls of the Bower. Did he remember what he had bellowed in the chapel, disrespectful before God, while inflamed with his desire? *I do swear that we shall be as husband and wife…*

Nodding, he glanced down, his eyes shadowed. "Yes…yes, it would make me happy too. But the time is not yet, Rosamund. You do understand, do you not? It is not easy, even for a King, to put a wife away, and I would wager Eleanor must decide to go herself; she will not retire gracefully just because I prefer your bed to hers."

"I understand." I took his hand in mine. "Now…do you?"

He heaved a great sigh. "Yes. You are as precious as any gem to me but I cannot keep you behind closed doors forever, for you are flesh and blood, not some lifeless jewel."

"Thank you, my Lord…my love." Kneeling, I kissed his hand in true gratitude.

He raised me and touched my cheek, then touched my mouth with his. His arm circled my waist, tight, proprietary. He nodded toward the bed with its broidered hangings. "My lady, let us make the most of the last moments we have before I must depart again."

So I had some freedom. I visited the nuns of Godstow and was pleased they still welcomed me despite my unorthodox lifestyle. I went to Oxford and bought cloth from the drapers and jewellery from the silversmiths and even books from the booksellers in Catte Street. Did the folk of Oxford guess that I was the King's mistress? As my chariot rolled into town, painted without device, I saw many of them stare, the women with a hint of envy and disdain, the men with rampant curiosity, even longing. I refused to meet the eyes of any onlooker, though, no matter how they stared; I assumed a demure and retiring manner, as if I were a properly wedded wife. The people, if they deduced my identity, would not be given cause to throw a charge of inconstancy at me; I was no whore like that lowborn woman, Ikenai, who had given Henry his bastard son, Geoffrey.

Once I caught a student in his gown, staring; he had long golden hair and a handsome face, and for just an instant, caught unaware by his sudden appearance in an arched doorway, our eyes met. His lips curved up, as though in great joy or wonder, as the Angelus bells in the priories and abbeys chimed out, and he murmured, just loud enough for me to hear, "*I who am struck are called Maria, the Rose of the World.*"

Did he speak of the bells, the Virgin or me? Blushing, I broke the unexpected meeting of our gazes, turned and hastened away into the teeming Oxford streets.

Henry was frequently out of the country on business but when he returned to England, he always fared to Woodstock to 'hunt.' Sometimes he *did* hunt, chasing the dappled deer through the nearby forests, but now he took me with him, riding by his side while his retainers quietly went about their business with no comment and no condemnation—at least not in words. Who would dare?

We hawked too, something I had enjoyed when I lived with my family on the Borders—and the King gave me a fine gyrfalcon called Ulysses. Passion still raged between us, in the woodlands with the servants far out of earshot, in the Bower with its wild topiary and copulating figures—but our union had grown and deepened beyond mere desires of the flesh. We had quiet times together, too, when Henry told me of the affairs of state and of matters that weighed heavy on his mind. His former friend Becket still irked him, for instance; the man was endlessly troublesome, unable to contain his mischief. Recently he had excommunicated Richard de Lucie, one of Henry's justiciars, and many others besides, for he feared they were trying to wrest the church's powers from his grasp.

"I am going to make sure Thomas submits to me," said Henry with fierce determination. We were in the great park at Woodstock, mounted on horseback, our hawks on our leather-clad wrists. "Sadly, Rosamund, this means I must leave England again. I will meet Becket at Montmirail."

"This time, I pray he see sense," I said.

"So do I," said Henry. "For I have other matters of import to deal with—the Coronation of my son Henry, the Young King, which shall take place in June."

"How extraordinary that he should be crowned while you live," I said. "Has it ever been done so in England?"

"I think not," replied Henry, "but it is a custom of the House of Capet in France and I think it a fine way to give a son some responsibility. It should keep young Henry out of trouble, and it will also make my intentions for the succession clear."

"I hope you are right," I sighed. All of us knew of the dangers of an uncertain accession; the land had suffered greatly because of the battles between King Stephen and Empress Matilda, who each believed the other had no right to rule.

"I am seldom wrong," said Henry with arrogance, and he loosed his hawk Nestor from his wrist, watching as the bird soared high into the sky to attack a smaller bird darting across the dome of heaven.

An avian shriek sounded from above and feathers drifted to the earth, spiralling down on capricious winds. Beak and talons bloody, Nestor returned to his master, bearing his mangled prey.

I had seen this same scenario so many times, the flight, the attack, the fall…but for some reason, on this day, it made my blood turn to ice.

A private courier reached the Tower, bearing grave news from France. After a brief reconciliation at Montmirail, during which Becket submitted to the King, negotiations had failed, with the Archbishop becoming insolent over his perceived rights. Still seeking to sweep away the ill will, Henry had arranged a second meeting at Leger-en-Yveline, but it only worsened the situation—as they wrangled over the council table, the two hard-headed men fell out spectacularly, shouting and roaring at each other until their attendants feared they might leap at each other's throats. Becket stormed out of the chamber, knocking aside those who sought to stop him with his crozier, and shortly thereafter a papal ultimatum was issued on the King. Henry was, understandably, furious. Involvement by the Pope brought a new, dangerous level to Henry's feud with Becket.

"Ah, I fear no good will come of this warring," I murmured, as I sat in the Tower with my ladies dressing my hair. "Why must Thomas Becket fight Henry every step of the way? It was the King who raised him to greatness!"

"But it is God's will that rules over all! Or should!" It was Juliana who spoke. She no longer dressed my hair, after our earlier confrontation over her attitude, but she still performed the rest of her duties in a clipped, vaguely aggressive manner—efficient but cold and slightly unnerving. Right now, she was in the corner of the chamber, brushing down one of my gowns and rubbing out marks as she prepared to hang it in the privy, where odours would kill any parasites that lurked in the folds. Her left hand, raw and red from the effort, was claw-like as it gripped the brush.

Blanche and Orable cast her warning looks but it seemed a fire burned within my least favourite tiring woman, loosening her tongue. Why she disliked me so, I did not know, for I had never once been unkind to her until she was cruel to me.

"If the King fights constantly with the Church, who knows where it will end for England?" Juliana cried, tossing her mousy-brown braid over her shoulder in an agitated motion. "If he sets himself up as if he has the powers of God Almighty, he may well end up excommunicated and the land placed under interdict. What would happen to us all?—Pain and suffering, just as the people endured during his mother's war!"

Blanche and Orable stared at the floor, unwilling to look at their ranting companion. Icy anger gripped me and I craned my head around to glare at Juliana. "You criticise your Lord King?" I said in a voice that was silken yet containing an edge of steel. "Remember by whose will you are here. And remember to whom you speak."

"Oh, I cannot forget *that*, my lady," Juliana said with clear sarcasm, her lip curling in an ugly sneer. Dropping my dress on the tiles like so much rubbish, she hurried toward the door.

"Where are you going?" queried Orable, her voice shaking.

"To lie down," Juliana flung over her shoulder. "I am not well. I feel sick…"

"We must go after her," Blanche glanced nervously at Orable.

"No, you will stay." Both ladies jumped as I spoke. I had almost reached the end of my endurance with Juliana. I was now mistress at the Tower, not just Henry's mistress. I wanted to be obeyed, as was expected in a noble household. I was no longer a young girl afraid and unsure in a strange environment. This, for good or for ill, was my home, my life.

"You will stay and we will do needlework together. Juliana may go, but only because I have no wish to see her sulky face for the rest of the day."

"Yes, my lady," Blanche and Orable squeaked in unison, sounding like a pair of frightened mice. I almost smiled but not quite—for Juliana and her unwarranted attitude lingered ever in my mind.

A few nights later a terrible thing happened, ripping my heart asunder like the claws of a wild beast, tearing away the veneer of happiness from my life at the Bower.

I had been in the labyrinth with Patch; the King had earlier sent his gardeners to plant several rose bushes around the periphery of Rosamund's Well. I went to examine them but found them lacking flowers and covered with curving thorns; as I bent forward to examine them, one caught my sleeve and tore a gaping hole in the fine silk.

Angry at my own clumsiness, I hurried back towards the Tower. My three women were in the hall, sewing, and were unaware that I had re-entered the building; they were not expecting me so soon, for I liked to take long walks during which I gathered my thoughts.

Up at the top of the stairs, I heard Orable chide: "You must be careful, Juliana. You must not push too far. The King pays you well, does he not?"

"Aye," Juliana responded. "But sometimes it becomes unbearable. The things he sends her…the jewels…the dresses. You'd think she was the Queen, not just some harlot!"

"She is obviously not just 'some harlot' to his Grace," said Orable primly. "I do not understand why you take against her. She is a kindly mistress. She does not beat us or make us toil from dawn to dusk. Hah, one would almost think you were jealous of her, Juliana!"

"Jealous!" cried Juliana. "Why should I be jealous of a trollop with hair red as Judas? It's not pretty; it befits a...a whore! What I cannot understand is why *her*? The King has plenty of others, Annabel de Balliol, a married Welshwoman called Nesta, and Alis de Porhoet. They say he seduced Alis when she was his ward; her father Lord Eudo complained bitterly to the King about the loss of her maidenhead! Ruined, he accounted her. All those fine ladies in his bed, and yet he gives the most attention to this spotted red wench from the Marches."

"You are most unfair," said Blanche, who was my favourite of my three personal servants. She spoke to me the most and seemed to have a kind heart. "His Grace is a lusty man; he is far from alone in that. And even a man of licentiousness may have his favourite...and even know love. I believe the King's Grace loves the Lady Rosamund dearly."

But Juliana's acid tongue would not be quelled. "Love? Pah! The King gives many gifts to his women—that's not love. Remember that overblown slattern called BelleBelle? He had garments made for her at the same time as he ordered gowns for the Queen. Did he love *her*? By Saint Agatha's Paps, half the lords in London have tumbled *that* one."

"But he prefers Rosamund above all the others, you said it yourself. He even prefers her above the Queen, who has recently been shipped off to Poitiers! You can see the adoration in his eyes when he gazes upon her. This is no passing fancy on his Grace's part; if it was, she would have been sent forth long ago."

"The Queen, the poor spurned Queen," said Juliana. "I feel sympathy for her—although often sluttish herself, nevertheless, she did her duty and gave him a fine pack of children. Rosamund cannot even do that, it would seem. For all their rolling about in that great big bed, nothing ever comes of it! She is a barren field; over ploughed, I dare say."

"I still say you seem jealous, Juliana," said Orable. "Did you hope to catch the King's eye yourself? Before you came to work here, I heard you were a servant at Woodstock Palace. Did you hope to catch Henry's eye then, get a little royal bastard in your belly, and perhaps win a pension out of it?"

There was a moment's silence, then, "I caught more than his eye, Orable. Fresh from the hunt, he came riding in to Woodstock once, laughing with the blood of the kill red upon him. His hair was tousled and his eyes burning; never, I swear, was a man so exciting as the King in that hour. Like any commoner, he stripped off his bloody shirt within the stable…and saw me standing there, watching him. It was as if lightning flared between us. He sent his squires away and he had me in the hay, blood on him and all. Never have I had a lover as lusty and skilled as the King! I had hoped he would summon for…sport…again, but it was never more than that once. Instead, I was passed over as if I did not exist, and the reason soon became clear—he brought *her* here, fresh from a convent, a pretty virgin child with an empty head."

"Not so empty," said Blanche. "And I think we should talk no more of this matter, Juliana."

Head reeling, I leant against the cold, sweating wall outside the hall. Bile burned the back of my throat. I cared not that Juliana hated me…but Henry…he had slept with her. With plain, sullen Juliana. *He had me in the hay…*

And those other women she had mentioned, Annabel, Nesta, Alis, and BelleBelle, of all names *BelleBelle*; they were clearly not women of his distant past, half-forgotten follies of his youth, but lemans of the present day, sharing Henry's bed even as I did. Filling in when Henry was far away from my bed in the turret room.

Gulping in great heaves of air, I gathered myself together and stepped into the hall. Blanche uttered a little shriek of horrified surprise and covered her mouth with a hand as if to try to hold back any more terrible secrets. Juliana jumped in fright and for all her harsh talk, went as white as milk. Then, her expression changed to one of defiance and she came at me, her chin outthrust defiantly. She was not a pretty girl, and I felt ill…What had possessed Henry to tumble such a one, lacking both comeliness and kindly nature?

"I suppose you heard…" she began. "I will not apologise!"

My voice grated out, hard as an old woman's. "That is up to you, Juliana. I make no apologies for what I do next either—I command that you leave the Tower at once and never return again."

Juliana's mouth gaped like that of a hooked fish. I shuddered, imagining Henry kissing that slack mouth as he rolled with her in the stables amidst the dung and the hay, probably watched by grinning stableboys hiding in the stalls. "You…you cannot! You did not hire me; the King brought me here. He is my master, not you…"

"I will write to him if you do not leave of your own volition," I warned. "I will tell him what you have revealed, of your dangerous jealousy. Do not think he will protect you just because he swived you once long ago. Christ, no doubt he has had more women than any of us have had hot meals; you are just one of those, used and then forgotten! He will punish you harshly for your waywardness rather than berate me for casting you out, of that I can assure you."

"You treacherous red bitch!" cried Juliana, her eyes welling up and a sob catching in her throat. "You believe yourself to be more than you are! One day it will all come back on you. The old Queen will decide she had enough and put an end to your ruination of her marriage."

My lips drew to thin lines. "I doubt she has her sights set on me. After all—Annabel, Alis, Nesta, and the delightfully named BelleBelle are all other contenders for Henry's affections, it would seem. But I tire of discussing this sordid matter. Get you gone, before I call the gate guard to have you thrown out."

Juliana stormed from the chamber, crashing and bashing about as she fled down the spiralling stairs into the kitchen and away through the servants' tunnel to the outside world.

Blanche and Orable stared at me, big-eyed, speechless. At length, Blanche licked her lips and said in the most humble tones, "Can we get you anything, mistress?"

"No," I said weakly, and turning from their sombre faces, I raced up to my own apartments, where I cast myself upon the bed I had shared with Henry and dampened the broidered coverlet with my tears.

The King was back in England for the Coronation of the Young King and on his way to Woodstock. Young Henry would stay at the Palace…and his father would come to me. I wondered if Young Henry knew of us, or cared; did he stand for his mother, or did he agree with his father's right to seek pleasure where he would? Perhaps neither—I had heard he was a self-centred lad who thought not too deeply beyond the next elaborate banquet or hunt. He was not even much concerned with his betrothed, Princess Margaret; he had left her in France and she would not be crowned with her husband—something I thought was a grave mistake.

I had my remaining two ladies dress me; I wore a gown of violet hue and a cloak the colour of starlight. As Henry was coming to me in private, I let my hair flow loose, running like a crimson ribbon over my shoulders to my waist.

I heard his footsteps on the stone stairs. Heavy, determined. I bit my lips, kept my head held high. How I longed to see him, and yet the names of other women churned in my brain, as they had done for months—Annabel, Nesta, Alis, BelleBelle….

Henry entered the chamber, looking windswept and tired. The torchlight caught on a silver hair in his beard. He glanced around. "No dog to bite me?"

I shook my head. "I sent her to the kitchen in care of the potboy. He gave her a nice bone full of marrow, I am told. I thought you would appreciate quiet and she is happy enough near the warm ovens."

"My Rosamund, so thoughtful towards me." He approached me like a huge bear, kicking the door shut behind him. He embraced me from behind, burying his face in my hair and cupping my breasts in his hands. I froze; desire flowed through me, a burst of delicious fire, but then…anger. Anger I was not entitled to—for I was but a concubine.

He must have felt me stiffen in his embrace. "What is wrong?" He let his arms drop to his sides and took a few paces back.

"I have dismissed Juliana," I said in a voice that came out flat.

"Why? What did she do…? Ah…" Henry suddenly bowed his head, clearly remembering what had once occurred between him and Juliana. He moved toward me, holding out his hands. "My beloved, why are you so upset? It was before we met, and it…it was a bit of a jest with my men. Who could find a willing wench to tup immediately after the hunt. I won, of course. I never thought of the creature again; indeed, I had more or less forgotten about that brief encounter when I hired the girl to assist you. She was always lurking around the palace and seemed to be able to keep her mouth shut."

"Not for long, not to me," I said bitterly. "And if you had forgotten Juliana, my lord, she clearly had not forgotten you. But it was not that rude bedding that pains me; as you say, it was long in the past, and she was nothing. But she told me the names of other recent mistresses of yours; and that you even have a new baby son with one."

"Ah little Morgan," said Henry. "A fine boy. But fear not, Rosamund; his mother Nesta is nothing like you, she is dark haired, dark eyed…"

"Like the Queen then," I said bitterly.

"Hardly!" he laughed. "Save that she has the same desire to 'sample' all the wealthy men she can lay her hands on. She is short and plump, like a little brown bird. Naughty…"

"I do not want to know such details…" I folded my arms defensively over my chest.

"As for Annabel and Alis…Well, they were both beautiful and willing. And you were far away. God's Teeth woman, I am not a saint and never will be. I cannot believe you are chastising me for being a man…when I am the King of England!"

There was a trace of anger in his tone now, but as emotions that had roiled within me for months burst to the fore, I cast caution to the wind. "Alis was supposed to be in your care, wasn't she? I've heard that her father was furious that you deflowered her!"

"He was…but I think I feared him less than you in your rage, woman!" Reaching out, he snatched hold of my wrists; he was not gentle. "Come, silence your tongue. You are the one I want above all others, whether you believe me or not."

"I must believe you…" Tears began, though I struggled to suppress them, "for if I do not truly have your love, what do I have? Your other women at least walk free and may marry or do as they will."

Henry stared at me and his eyes suddenly blackened with wrath. He let out a roar. "I have said it before, you are not my prisoner! I have allowed you more freedoms, have I not? If you truly think you are hard done by, go…go now to the old hags in the convent of Godstow!"

"See?" I cried, tears slipping from the corners of my eyes. "Even as you say I can go, you want me to go somewhere else where I would be shut in. Locked within a cloister, bound to eternal chastity. What if I said I wanted my freedom so that I could marry?"

He shook his head; his expression was full of danger. I tormented him with my words as one might bait a bear. But unlike the bears in the bear-pits in town and castle, he had no chains to shackle him. He could attack. "I will never let any other man have you, Rosamund. Never. We will be together until one or other of us is dead. Do you hear me? And if it is a wife you wish to be; it may happen, but you must be patient! These things take time."

I fell silent. "Do you truly mean it?"

"How can you still doubt me? I said it before the altar on our first night together, did I not? I already consider you my wife, Rosamund. Let me tell you…Eleanor and I do not sleep together anymore. She is more interested in her sons than in me. Since John's birth, we have been like brother and sister—warring siblings!"

I gazed into his face, his angry, tortured face. Did I believe him? "What will you do?"

"For the moment, nothing. My son's upcoming Coronation takes precedence and I must also see my boy Richard invested in Aquitaine and Geoffrey in Brittany. I fear Becket may yet cause me more grief too; these things must come before my heart's desire. When the day comes…Well, Eleanor squeezed out of her marriage to Louis of France due to consanguinity. As it happens, she and I are similarly related. I can try that angle to rid myself of her but…it is not so easy as just letting her go. I will not mourn if Eleanor goes but there are other considerations…"

"But you want what she brought to the marriage. You want Aquitaine."

"Yes."

"She will fight you."

"Yes. Tooth and nail most likely. But I will win."

You do not know women as well as you think you do, Henry…I pray you are right."

"I *am* right. I am the King. So…happier now?" He reached out and wiped a tear from my cheek with his thumb.

"Yes," I said. It was not entirely the truth but I knew he would give short shrift to continued tears and melancholy.

"Come, smile at me, sweeting, we must not waste the short time we have together." He pulled me slowly but firmly towards the bed.

"Always so short a time together…I wish I could come to London with you," I said. "I would love to see Westminster."

He paused in the middle of lifting my skirts. His hand was fire on the inside of my thigh. "Well, maybe that could be arranged. The Queen is remaining in Poitiers….Damn it to hell, why not? You must remain a spectator, naturally."

He began to kiss my shoulder, as my dress and under-garments came over my head and were discarded. "Christ, I had forgotten how splendid you are, woman."

"One thing you must promise me," I gasped, as he seized hold of me, not gentle but possessive, demanding, and pushed me against the bolster, struggling with the ties of his own clothes.

"What is that, my beloved?" His voice was muffled as he buried his face against my bare flesh, the rough hairs on his chin making me tingle with growing desire.

"Promise me that BelleBelle won't be there. BelleBelle with her fancy dress!"

"BelleBelle!" Henry loosed a huge laugh, and his hand came down on my buttock in a playful swipe. "I promise you, Rosamund Clifford, that mistress BelleBelle will be nowhere near Westminster and your dress will be a thousand times better than any rag I ever gave to her!"

The day of Henry the Young King's Coronation drew near. After a damp, rain-washed May, when winds ripped the blossoms from the trees, June was an unexpected delight; the sun blazed in an azure sky and heat waves rippled over the fields. Excitement made me giddy as I set out in my unmarked chariot with Blanche attending me and guards sent by Henry watching at front and rear.

Once away from the Tower, Blanche seemed brighter and chattier than usual. "It will be a splendid occasion!" she remarked. "And you, my lady, you will look splendid too. I am sure all eyes will be upon you at the Young King's feast!"

"I pray not!" I said, suddenly worried. "I am sure that would not be the King's intention."

Blanche must have seen my frown. "No sense in fretting about it, my Lady. The King has asked for you to be there, so there you shall be. We will be careful, though. Careful and discreet."

It seemed to take an eternity to reach London, and by the time we arrived at the city gates our initial enthusiasm was waning. Blanche and I were hot and dusty, sweating in the summer heat and desirous of a bath and a drink. Having little else to do, we had polished off a parcel of sweetmeats and marchpane and that, combined with the rocking of the chariot over the rutted roads, had made us feel quite sick. Every now and then, we peered out the window to get some air and see the sights—the huge walls and gates, the churches with their battlemented towers, the merry throng of revellers parading through the streets.

"Ah, what is that smell?" Blanche suddenly paled and pressed a kerchief to her nose.

I twitched aside the velvet curtain that hung over the chariot window—and gasped in horror. Not ten feet away was a row of severed heads on pikes, rotting in the heat. Some were little more than skulls, the flesh ripped off by voracious gulls; others were more recent, with green, livid flesh and gaping mouths. I let the curtain fall, my hands trembling and bile rushing into my mouth.

"Don't look, Blanche, don't look!" I ordered.

She put her hands over her mouth and retched. "I don't need to look! Only one thing smells both sweet and foul at once!"

The chariot rolled on, while Blanche and I continued to choke and gag, the scent of decay lingering in our nostrils. I felt dismayed. I knew the sheriffs and justices frequently displayed the body parts of criminals in towns across the land to exhort the citizens to uphold the law, but I had never been exposed to such horrors in my young life. It made me realise how Tower and Bower shielded me from a world that was harsh and violent, even deadly.

Blanche and I were driven to Kilchurn priory, where accommodation with the nuns had been arranged. The priory was a small, intimate religious house founded over forty years before for Christina, Emma and Gunhilda, the three loyal ladies-in-waiting of old Queen Consort Matilda, the King's grandmother. After the Queen's death, they had retired to Kilchurn, living in a hermitage near a holy spring until the Bishop of London approved the foundation of a nunnery.

Exhausted, we settled into the nuns' guesthouse and the sisters brought us bread, wine, and ewers of water to wash in. The sun sank and beyond the arched windows of the priory, the sky blazed red and turned all the needle-like spires of London to blood.

"It looks very fair now," said Blanche, gazing out. "Red as rubies. It will dawn a fair day for the Young King's Coronation. Orable will be so jealous, being left behind in the Tower."

"I will seek out a present for her while we are in London," I said, watching the last of the sunlight slip away and the crimson sky turn the colour of wine, deep and rich. The stars came out, glittering like gems, and a red round moon soared over London, a watchful eye looking down on king and commoner alike, spying on taverns and brothels and mansions and monasteries. Somewhere in the growing velvety darkness, an unseen musician was playing a jaunty air on a flute.

I wondered where Henry stayed that night, and what merriment he indulged in with his closest friends. I sighed; perhaps it was best not to know. The King was what he was, and he would never change. It was some consolation he had wanted me here, on the important occasion of his son's Coronation.

He had asked me to come when he could have denied me utterly. Where, for example, was the fair Annabel de Balliol? It was a small, but important victory.

The next day we gathered outside Westminster, under the stretching blue shadow of the huge abbey. Blanche and I had places prepared for us, near to the great west doors; I could see men glancing over at me, wondering who I was. After my jibe about BelleBelle and her gown, Henry had duly sent me a fine outfit to wear for the Coronation. Silver tissue, pale as moonlight, frothed to my ankles, the long sleeves and hem awash with seed pearls. Over it, I wore a summer cloak of rare violet hue, its hood lined with marten fur and its edges gleaming with golden threads each as fine as a hair. A necklace which bore two rubies flanking an emerald clasped my throat and on my hair, worn loose as I was not a married woman (at least not in any way others would accept) there lay a silver circlet.

Blanche was fanning her face with her hand; even though it was before noon, the day was sweltering, the discomfort fuelled by the constant press of crowds around the Abbey. The air was so hot it shimmered; and it reeked, too—not with the scent of the severed heads of criminals, but with the odour of the nearby Thames which, sunk low in its winding course, revealed to men's eyes (and to their offended noses!) rotting ship-hulks, rotting ordure, rotting carcasses; all the sunken detritus of the ancient city.

"I hope this won't take too long," Blanche said, clearly in some distress. "I think I might faint. I would be so humiliated if I fell down when others might see."

"Have strength, Blanche," I held her arm in what I hoped was a comforting way.

At that moment, a trumpet blared, its notes bouncing back and forth between the towering façade of the Abbey and the clustered buildings behind, all garlanded in bright banners. The crowd thrust forward again, and people were calling out, "The old King is coming…and the new! Young Henry is coming with his father!"

The trumpet roared again, and many others joined it. The tall doors of the Abbey parted just as Christ parted the waters of the sea and a rush of incense-laden air swelled out to wash over us. The lords of the land began to appear in our sightlines, marching steadfastly towards Westminster whilst carrying the swords of state, the sunlight glinting off their tips and jewelled hilts. A bevy of Bishops processed after them, Jocelyn of Salisbury, Walter of Rochester, Hugh of Durham, Gilbert of London and many others, accompanied by Giles de Evreaux and Henry de Bayeaux, a pair of visiting Bishops from Normandy, distinguished from the English ones by their different standards. The Archbishop of York, Roger Pont l'Eveque, walked after them on the red carpet rolled out from the Abbey door for he would be the one to perform the ceremony—a controversial act, for normally it was the prerogative of the Archbishop of Canterbury to crown an English monarch. But Becket was still overseas and out of favour, despite the recent muting of hostilities with the King.

Narrowing my eyes against the glare of the sun, I scanned the haughty, stern features of Pont l'Eveque, a mysterious man tainted by scandal. When he was but a youthful clerk, a lad named Walter claimed Roger had committed unnatural vices upon his person. Pont l'Eveque denied all and began a judicial case for slander against his former friend, and it did not end well for Walter—the boy lost the case and his eyes were put out. Not to be deterred, the blinded Walter pressed charges against l'Eveque, but wealthy and persuasive Roger bought off the judges and saw that Walter was silenced forever…by being hung by the neck till he died.

Today, though, there was no sign of that violent, sinful youth of long ago. In his gleaming alb, dalmatic and mitre, Pont l'Eveque truly looked the part of a man of God, one ready to make history at this Coronation—for not only was it unheard of that an Archbishop of York crowned a King, it was also the first time in England that a prince became monarch while his father lived. Such was a custom of the Capets of France, and Henry was insistent on importing it.

Yet another trumpet sounded, high-pitched and joyous. The young King himself was striding down the red carpet, clad in the traditional dalmatic, *tunicle* and cope. Shielding him from the burning sun, his attendants lifted a canopy of cloth of gold over his head.

I rose on the tips of my toes to look at him—the fruit of Henry and Eleanor's union. He was tall—taller than his father, who was rather stocky—with shining red-gold curls to his shoulders and a fair, pale-skinned young face liberally dotted with freckles. A little needle of sorrow stabbed into me; with his reddish hair and pale skin, he could have almost been our son, had Henry never wed the woman from Aquitaine…

Then the Young King swept past, the crowd gaping and gawking at his beauty and screaming his name, and Henry himself appeared, bare-headed, clad in ermine and robes of white samite. He followed in his son's wake with serious yet proud demeanour.

I stood still as a stone as he walked past me, scarcely ten feet away. In a moment of perversity, I willed him to look at me—but he did not. He was fixated upon his duty as father and King. Head held high, he followed the procession of clergy and nobles into the candlelit interior of Westminster Abbey. The doors closed.

I was so near, and there at his invitation…and yet, no matter what had passed between us, the door was still shut.

Inside, the great organ boomed out, its music soaring to heaven. *Ta Deum.*

Blanche and I returned to our accommodation at Kilchurn Priory. We spent two more days in London, visiting goldsmiths and silversmiths and the drapers and spice merchants and other culinary items not available in the Oxford market to carry back to our cook.

All over the city, men spoke of the Young King's Coronation: '*He put his hands upon the altar and swore to uphold Mother Church! He'll be a true lord to us, I deem!*' and of the grand banquet at Westminster Palace after: '*The Old King himself bore the first course, a mighty boar's head, to the high table and placed it humbly before the new King. Never seen that happen before!*'

But not all the talk was of happy events. Apparently, when Henry set the boar's head on its silver platter before his son, he had said jovially, "It is unusual for a prince to be served by a King!" Young Henry, already imbibing copious quantities of wine and surrounded by pompous young nobles of his retinue, had stared down his nose at his father and returned, "Aye, but it is nothing unusual about a mere count serving a King!" referring, with great rudeness, to his father's former title of Count of Anjou.

Henry had laughed off his son's 'wit' but I thought the tone insolent and disrespectful, especially as Henry need not have chosen to crown his son and could have let the boy battle out the succession with his brothers Geoffrey, Richard and John. I did not think the Young King's attitude augured well for the future.

Men talked too of how Young Henry had rushed to England for his Coronation and forgotten his long-termed betrothed, Margaret of France. By all rights, she should have been crowned with him, and rumour had it her father was furious.

"Where will it all end?" said Blanche mournfully. "I hope there will not be war with France."

"I doubt it will come to that." I shook my head, but a growing unease gripped me. Something felt wrong—the wrong Archbishop crowning the Young King, the exclusion of Princess Margaret, the insolence of young Henry to his father at the banquet. In fact, the whole

Coronation, with a King crowned while his sire lived, a tradition not that of England's monarchs, seemed somehow *wrong*.

Despite the heat of the day, I shivered. "We should go home soon, Blanche. As soon as possible. The King has not sent word to me or asked me to come into his presence…"

My voice trailed off and I caught Blanche looking at me with an expression akin to pity.

"He…he must be busy," I stammered, reddening. "There is much for him to do here, in the aftermath of the Coronation."

"I am sure he is very busy." Blanche patted my arm. "I think you are right; it is better that we should go."

The decision was made. Our baggage packed, we climbed into the unmarked chariot that everyone had stared at and whispered about when we first arrived in London. Having lost interest in the grandeur of the Coronation, the locals had ceased staring now. Most were too head-sore after imbibing the free wine that had flowed through the conduits for several days—a gift from the Young King and from Henry.

We rolled away and as we passed the city wall, the wind of our gathering speed blew the draperies on the carriage back and I saw the line of severed heads again. They grinned, grimaced, the birds flocking around them, their hair torn asunder like cobwebs on the rising wind—a reminder of how death was all around us, even as we lived.

For the first time in my life, I felt truly afraid. All of Henry's warnings about Eleanor's wrath had fallen on the deaf, foolish ears of a wilful girl but now I saw, in those heads that once laughed, loved, and breathed, how easily it could be done. How the life thread could be snipped…just like that….

Then the grotesque mementoes of life, of death, were gone, lost from sight amidst carts and foot soldiers and merchants filing in and out of the city gates, and I travelled on with a silent Blanche reclining at my side. I found myself glad to be out of London's stink and bustle; to be able to smell the sweet scents of fields and trees and feel the clean wind from the west upon my face.

When we reached our destination several days hence, surprisingly and unexpectedly, my heart leapt to see the Tower pointing up into the sky, and I realised with a shock that this place, which I had once thought of as a prison, was now a sanctuary, a safe haven holding out the evil world. No longer threatening and sinister, it was *home*.

As the chariot rumbled to a halt deep within the stand of trees outside Woodstock's walls, the sky above darkened and thunder began to rumble. The heat that had lain over England had broken. A storm was coming.

"Run, mistress Rosamund!" cried Blanche, as a flash of lightning lit the shadowed spaces beneath the waving trees and rain started to flood down in watery sheets. Another boom of thunder rolled overhead, shaking the earth below, and a fork of lightning descended from the heavens, smiting an old, blighted oak on the edge of the grove. The dried-out wood burst into flames and the air reeked of sulphur, foetid as the pits of Hell.

Blanche and I shrieked and rushed for the safety of the tunnel that led into the Bower and Tower. Wet, dripping, hearts pounding, we stumbled in the half-lit gloom, grappling with the key to permit us entry to each level.

When at last we reached the hall, we fell down, breathless, drenched, laughing with nervous excitement. "We made it," said Blanche, as outside the storm roared like an angry giant and wind battered the Tower.

I stumbled to the window and glanced out. The sky was a bruise, the topiary in the labyrinth blowing back and forth, back and forth. The heads of the roses planted by the well were disintegrating in the violent gusts and petals eddied through the turbulent air.

"Yes, we are safe," I whispered, as much to myself as to Blanche. "Here, we can surely weather any storms that strike us."

Henry had departed England for Normandy and the tidings couriers brought from abroad ranged from disturbing to gratifying. Thomas Becket had risen in wrath over the matter of the Young King's Coronation. In high dudgeon because the Archbishop of York officiated at the ceremony instead of Canterbury, he complained bitterly to the Pope that his right had been usurped—and the Pope had granted him permission to place England under Interdict if Becket decided that it would be fitting.

So concerned was Henry that he stifled his rage at his one-time friend and agreed to treat with Becket. Once again, a peaceful agreement seemed to have been reached between them; beneath their differences, a spark of brotherliness still existed. There would be no interdict. The people of England could rest easy, knowing that their children would be baptised and the dead buried with respect. Thomas Becket would return home to Canterbury and resume his role as Archbishop.

"I am glad to hear that Becket's mad plans have been thwarted," said Orable, as she toyed with her needlework. "Whatever is wrong with the man? He thinks he is King amongst bishops!"

I shook my head. "I do not know. Some men are like that when they gain power—they want more and more, until it becomes an all-consuming obsession. I just pray that Henry will return to England soon, now that a true reconciliation has taken place."

"I pray so too, my lady," said Blanche. She glanced at me out of the corner of her eye; she had noticed me growing fretful over the past few weeks and guessed the reason why. I had heard nothing from the King since the Coronation in London. The news that had arrived was impersonal, sent to the household and not to me.

But Henry did not come. Long weeks stretched into months. The money for wages and maintenance arrived, as it always did, and we wanted for nothing at the Tower…but no personal messages came from Henry. Black despair blossomed in my heart and I imagined many unhappy possibilities. Perhaps he had reconciled with Eleanor. Or had found a buxom French mistress or two. Or three. Maybe my time was over, and I was living a lie.

Then, finally, a letter arrived, bound and sealed. With a mixture of both eagerness and trepidation, I ripped it open. My heart sank as I pored over the letter's contents, and yet a warm glow of gladness rushed through me too. Henry had not forgotten me, and his words were full of affection!

Dear Heart, the letter read in Henry's own hand. *It was my intent to be in England by now but this business with Thomas Becket has flared up again. God curse him, Rosamund, it seems he wilfully sets out to needle and defy me…(*Here the ink was smudged, Henry's anger taking hold*.) Tidings may not have reached you at Woodstock but he has excommunicated all the Bishops that attended my son's Coronation! He smiled to my face then thrust a dagger into my back the moment he set sail for Canterbury. I will confer with my lords over the Christmas season on best how to deal with this fractious priest. When the winter storms have ceased and the tides turn favourable, I will return to you. Empty am I without your presence. Burn this letter, I bid you. Your Lover, H. Rex.*

Tears rushing to my eyes, I crumpled up the parchment and flung it in the fire. Blanche, busy brushing my gowns, glanced over. "Is everything all right, my Lady?"

"Yes and no…" I replied. I was relieved that Henry remembered me so fondly, but the news of Becket's latest rebellion filled my heart with an unknown dread.

Something was going to happen. I could feel it. It was uncomfortable, like a breath held too long until the lungs felt ready to burst. A sensation I could only imagine was like drowning…

I began to pace the floor of my apartments while my little dog, Patch, distressed by my agitation, worried at the hem of my gown.

Christmas flew by without much cheer. The Feast of the Innocents, when Herod slew the boy babies in an attempt to kill the Christ-child, came and went, virtually unmarked in our quiet existence, with only Father Morland to say masses and quiet prayers on that day deemed both unlucky and yet festive. No Boy Bishops presided at Rosamund's Bower, turning the world upside down for a day. Patch chewed bones and his mistress walked the maze.

Early in January it began to sleet, a mix of snow and rain that did not stick to roofs or walls but slapped against one's face like an open hand. By the month's end, it turned colder and a grey sky dumped its white waste over England.

Locked at the heart of that frigid world, I felt restive, charged with a strange, unhealthy energy. Wrapping up warmly and ignoring Blanche's protests that I should recline by the fire, I wandered alone into the Bower, walking widdershins around the twisted paths of the great labyrinth Henry had constructed. The green bushes with their fantastical shapes reared up like frozen monsters; the well Henry had named after me lay frozen and clogged with the rotting remnants of autumn leaves.

I knelt beside the well, sheltering from the lash of the wind within its stone embrasure. The nearby rose bushes were waving, denuded of all leaves and flowers; suddenly one frond lashed out, sharp as a whip, and its thorn caught my arm. I cried out as red jewels blossomed on my wrist and tumbled to pattern the snow with crimson.

I tore my arm free of the encircling vine, cradling it against my body—and then I heard the bells ringing, tolling out across the winter-smitten land, bells from the local villages and from the great tall towers of Woodstock Palace. Bells, bells, *bells...*

They were not joyous bells, like the bells of Christmas of Epiphany. They were not even the stolid, sedate bells that sounded from church towers on a Sunday. They were clanging and clashing in discordant cacophony—ringing out a warning, a message. I did not want to know what that message might be. Fire. Flood. Wolves. Winter. Death...Death of a person of importance, death that would bring dire consequences to England...and maybe to me.

Thrusting horrid visions from my mind, I raced towards the Tower, still clutching my wounded arm, the blood droplets dappling my dress. As I began to ascend the stairs, Blanche appeared at the top, gesturing frantically. "My Lady, you must go to your apartments and bolt the door!"

"Why? What is happening?" I glanced around wildly.

"You've heard the bells?"

"Yes, and I have deduced, as any sensible person might, that they betoken some evil. But...but..."

"There are men without the Tower," said Blanche in a trembling voice. "I will show you."

Grasping my sleeve, she dragged me up the stairs to the main hall, locked the door behind us, then rushed to the window embrasure. Carefully she unfastened one painted shutter, just a crack; fear made her slender fingers shake like an old woman's.

I leant into the embrasure, gazing out through the narrow slit. Sure enough, beyond the Bower, beyond the stout walls with no door, men on horseback were riding madly over the white drifts of snow, black shapes that seemed the very image of death horsed, some Biblical scene betokening the Apocalypse.

"I fear what news these riders bring," I moaned, my mouth going dry. "Yet...yet...I should wait and find out...It can only be death...doom..." My eyes went foggy and my head whirled. Jesu, Henry was not a young man and he had many enemies as most powerful men do. Maybe an assassin had attacked him or maybe a natural disaster had befallen—a tumble from a steed, a tertian fever. *Oh Christ and the Virgin, what would I do if Henry were dead...?*

"Lady, you must go to your room; I will deal with these strangers. It may not be what you think. There may be danger...to you. You know what the King's orders are. You must lock yourself in and bar the door. Go upstairs, I beg you, Rosamund."

"I will stay *here*, Blanche!" I cried, stamping my foot like a child, although it was terror rather than petulance that made me behave so. "You cannot make me go."

Outside the walls, I heard muffled shouts as the riders engaged in conversation with the guardians of the Bower. Strive as I might, I could not make out any of the words, so had no idea whether they might be friend or foe.

On the floor below, the kitchen level, there was a resounding bang as the hatch from the servants' private tunnel slammed open onto the floor. Metal-shod feet struck the kitchen tiles; Patch, ousted from his usual place near the ovens, was barking furiously at the newcomers. Voices rose, frightened, querying. The strangers were within!

I took a deep breath. I could put several doors between the intruders and myself, but what was the purpose if there was news I needed to hear. Danger or no, I had to find out the truth.

"Open the door," I said, nodding towards the locked door leading back downstairs. "I command you, Blanche."

"Oh, my Lady..." Blanche's teeth chattered and not from the cold as she fumbled at her belt, finding her precious key before thrusting it into the lock. The door swung open and the torches behind swirled and dipped as a bevy of darkly cloaked, mailed men mounted the top steps and entered the room, followed by the stout figure of the cook.

Cook bore a worried expression and clutched his hat in his hand. "Forgive me for disturbing you, my lady. I know we are breaking all the rules set out by his Grace…but…but these folks are here on important business. I think there is sommat you need to know, Lady Rosamund."

I tried to draw myself up haughtily, to look stern and serene in the face of disaster; inside I was withering. Henry was dead or ill or a prisoner…I knew it. He was dead and these men were here to remove me, and if they were from a vengeful widowed Queen, maybe remove me from the very earth, not just the Tower near Woodstock.

"Speak!" I ordered the men who faced me, their faces blotched from the perishing cold, their boots clogged with mud and their cloaks limp on their shoulders.

The leader stepped forward, bowed solemnly. "My Lady Clifford, a terrible thing has occurred."

I tried to keep my composure. "I gather that. I heard the bells toll. But first, tell me, whom do you serve? Where do you hail from?"

"I serve the King above all. My name is Berneval. However, I do not come from the King on this mission. I come because all men and woman, in all places across England, need to hear my tidings. What I have to say may be of particular interest to those…*close*…to his Grace the King."

"Then do not keep me waiting, sir. I wish to know your tidings."

"There has been a great tragedy."

I squared my shoulders, waiting for the words that would destroy my life.

"The Archbishop of Canterbury is dead."

I stared, not believing what I had heard. *Not the King.* Oh Jesu, thank you, not my Henry…

But Thomas Becket? He had always seemed hale and hearty. Too much so for a man of the cloth.

"It is a sorrowful occasion, certainly, when such a great man dies…" I said to the messenger Berneval. "May God have mercy on the Archbishop's soul! But…I am perplexed. Why have you come here in this manner to tell me? If you serve the King, you know he wishes but few to enter this dwelling."

Berneval bit his chapped lips and gazed down at the flagstones. "I realise that, my Lady, but…there is no easy way to say it… Archbishop Becket was murdered in Canterbury Cathedral as he prepared to attend Vespers. Four knights, Reginald FitzUrse, Hugh de

Morville, William de Tracy and Richard le Breton confronted him and ordered him to come to Winchester as their prisoner. When he refused, they drew their weapons and cut him down on the stairs leading to the quire."

Berneval swallowed, clearly upset. "Three blows it took to fell him; he went down on hands and knees, crying that he welcomed death. Then one of the knights struck him again, as he lay sprawled upon the floor and that blow sheared off the crown of his head, spilling his brains across the pavement of that holy place…"

The man before me began to weep, overcome by the horror of the tale he told. "At the last, one of the murderers' accomplices, a treacherous clerk, stepped upon Becket's neck and, forgive me for imparting such vileness, the miscreant scattered blood and brain matter over the floor. And he laughed shamefully and said to his fellows, "Let us be off! This priest will rise no more!" Whereupon the knights rode away and to this day they have not been apprehended."

"A terrible tale to be sure, but…but why…why? There is more, isn't there?"

"Lady…" Berneval gazed straight into my eyes, "the knights who killed Becket travelled by fastest ship from France. Their orders came from the King."

I started in shock, my gasp audible. My sovereign, my lover, had murdered a priest.

It was still winter, but spring showed the faintest signs of returning. A little more blueness in the sky, a little more warmth in the sun.

I felt no warmth as I walked, lonely, in the labyrinth. No more missives from Henry had reached me and the land was still abuzz with the horror of Thomas Becket's murder. The knights who had slain the Archbishop had seemingly escaped justice; they had fled from the castle of Ranulf le Broc, the very man who had brought me to Woodstock, to Knaresborough Castle in the north of England, where they were holed up like rats within the adamant keep.

I wondered what would become of me. The usual monies were still paid into the accounts of the estate, but I knew that gossip abounded in the kitchens that payments might soon cease, and even Orable wistfully mulled over what she might do 'if her services were no longer required.'

Suddenly I heard the crunch of boots on gravel. The gardeners had been cutting the overgrowth before it burgeoned outwards during the spring, and I assumed they were still busy within the Bower. Annoyed, I refused to look over my shoulder; I did not want anyone to witness my misery and give fuel to more rumours. Lifting my heavy skirts, I darted between several of the topiary figures and secreted myself in an alcove carved into a prickly hedge that remained verdant through the winter.

Sighing, I settled myself amidst the greenery, waiting for the gardeners to pass by on their way back to the Tower. Instead, a burly black figure filled the doorway, blotting out what little light there was, stance containing a powerful menace.

I let out a little involuntary cry. What a fool I had been not to have looked at who was behind me. An intruder! Someone had breached the Tower and Bower, and now…

I made to scream; a hand clamped over my mouth, stifling my cry. I bit down, my teeth sinking into a palm…

"Ah…you stupid wench, you've bitten me…" The tooth-marked hand was whipped away. Your stupid dog tried to savage me once; now you have. What ails you, Rosamund…after all this time, do you not recognise your own lord?"

I knew the voice at once. "Henry!" I cried. "You're here!"

He grasped my arm, pulled me out from the treed niche into the daylight. The King had aged greatly since I last saw him. Dark crescents underscored his eyes and new lines of worry creased his brow. Grey glittered in hair and beard.

"Your poor hand, forgive me..." I said, taking his wounded hand, red with the marks of my teeth, and kissing it. How warm and alive that hand felt...but... it was the hand of a killer. A slayer of priests.

A sudden trembling took me and I let his hand fall. Bowing my head, I stood before him, unable to meet his gaze.

"Rosamund, you do not look at me, you greet me with no kiss." His voice was harsh, gravelly. "What ails you? Have you..." His features began to redden; I knew one of his infamous Plantagenet rages was boiling up. "Have you listened to the lies they tell about me? Do you believe I have holy blood on my hands?"

I did not answer. I knew he was a great and powerful King, and ruthless when he needed to be. His involvement in Becket's death was not to be doubted; after all, it was an official court messenger who had informed me of the Archbishop's fate.

"How could you betray me? Everyone betrays me!" Henry shouted, waving his arms furiously in the air. He punched the bush next to him; it exploded in a shower of leaves, berries and twigs. "It was not as you think, Rosamund, I swear it!"

I forced myself to speak, despite the fact that his rages frightened me, and I assumed it was during one of those rages he had doomed the Archbishop. "A messenger came here, Henry. He told me you had ordered the death."

"Did he now?" Henry snarled. "Like all of them, all the fools, he interpreted what he thought had happened—and got it wrong. And who sent him, who? The land is full of mischief-makers! For all his meddling, all his bloody threats and unlawful excommunications, I did not want Thomas Becket to die! Do you not believe me?"

"I want to believe you, I want naught more! But knowing how he defied you and knowing your temper... If what I have heard is not true, Henry, I bid you tell me what *the truth is*!"

Henry was gnashing his teeth; not a good sign. "Questioned by a woman. My bloody bedmate, who is not even my wife! How low have I sunk? But yes, I will tell you and if you do not accept my words, I want you gone...gone from here, gone to Hell if it please you!"

Tears sprang to my eyes; I blinked them back. "Convince me, then! I am no shrew niggling you with inane questions about infidelities or other trivialities…I ask you here about the murder of an archbishop. A murder that all the country places at your door."

He gripped my wrists, pulled me to him. Words burst from his mouth, short, sharp, staccato. "I. Did. Not. Order. His. Death."

"What did happen then? You must tell me!"

Henry's eyes were wild with memories, almost starting from his head. He looked nigh on a madman. "It was late at night. A messenger came to my castle in Normandy with the news of Becket's latest antics. I was half-asleep, freezing cold, raging at his betrayal…all at once. I was in my nightshirt, for Christ's sake, standing in the hall with all my vassals staggering in from their own beds, staring at me. I looked a fool, I felt a fool! And it was all Becket's fault. My anger rose; you know how it can consume me…"

"Yes," I said softly. I was standing close to him now, touching him, then leaning against his chest, my arms locked around his broad frame. I could hear his heart hammering and feel that he was…trembling. The great and terrible King of England was shaking with pent up emotion and I suspected not all of it was from anger.

"I glanced around me, at all those faces; I fancied many of them mocked me. A King who could not contain a wily, out of control churchman. Rage flooded me and I shouted, 'What sluggards, what cowards have I allowed in my court, who care nothing for their allegiance to their lord! Who will rid me of this meddlesome priest?'

"And can you guess what happened then my beloved, my Rosamund?" The level of his voice dropped, the anger draining from him, though the sorrow still lingered. He released my wrists and let one finger trail along my cheek, wiping away the tears.

"Yes, Henry, I can," I whispered. "I think I know."

"Four knights seeking to curry my favour slipped out of the hall as I raved. They rode like the wind for the port and took the first available ship to England. The rest you know."

I closed my eyes. "You did not truly encompass Becket's death."

"I did not; I swear it on Christ's Cross. But it *is* my fault, Rosamund. I do not blame the knights who misconstrued my words."

"Why should you take the blame and they take none? They still did the deed and with great violence too, uncaring of the sanctity of the cathedral!" I cried. "They should be punished!"

"No…no punishment. Let God punish them when the time comes. I will take all the blame and I will do the penance for the act… They will make a saint of him, you know. Thomas. He will be more powerful in death than ever he was in life. Already people say miracles have occurred at the spot where he died, and charlatans in Canterbury market sell rags reddened with cow's blood as cloths that soaked up Thomas's blood from the floor!"

We began walking slowly back towards the Tower. Henry was grey-faced, yet the tension had gone out of him; he had unburdened himself and his anger was spent. "I will take the punishment, Rosamund," he said, "I have vowed to do so. And…" He clasped my hand again and slipped a ring upon it, with an emerald large as a pigeon's egg, a twin to the ruby he gave me long ago, before we were even truly lovers. "I also vow that you and I shall spend more time together. And that soon…soon…I will free myself of the ties that bind me. Just now, it would not be a good time to cause further grievance with the Church."

I knew he spoke of ridding himself of Eleanor of Aquitaine; my cheeks burned. "You no longer want me to 'go to Hell' then?"

"No, forgive me my foolish outburst! Rosamund Clifford, if it were up to me I would bear you from this place to Westminster this very day, and place you on a throne. But it cannot be done. Yet."

He bowed over me and enfolded me in his strong, sword-scarred arms. His mouth met mine hungrily, and neither of us cared that there might be watchers from the kitchen level or the hall.

That night our lovemaking was different—passionate and yet more tender than in the past. And at one point, as he dozed afterwards, Henry cried out Becket's name in his sleep, and I pulled him in close to me, and rocked him to sleep like a babe.

Henry grieved greatly for Becket and threw himself into a flurry of activities to ease the pain and guilt in his heart. Sometimes these activities took him far from England's shores, such as when he journeyed to Brittany upon the death of old Count Conan, to see his son Geoffrey take the Count's place. I loathed those times and longed for his return; I worried for him, for he seemed so lost and broken since the murder of Thomas Becket.

He returned to England in August and spent pleasant idle days with me at the Bower and at Woodstock, where we hunted, feasted and made love.

Happiness never seemed to last, alas. Word reached Henry that the Irish had invited his friend Richard de Clare, known as Strongbow, to be King of Leinster. Henry had sent Richard there, in his service, but had not anticipated de Clare might desire a higher position—an Irish crown.

"I cannot believe it, Rosamund!" Henry slammed his ring-laden hand on the table, making the silver goblets and dishes bounce. He had started telling me much of his policy of late—as he had, I supposed, once done with Eleanor when they were first wed, a young man with an older, worldly-wise woman interested in politics. I tried to be attentive, to match my rival in intellect. "I treated Richard like family. His mother was a mistress of my grandfather, Henry First, and for all I know Richard might actually *be* family. I never thought he would try to set himself up as a petty king. He has even managed to arrange a marriage with the daughter of the chieftain Dermot McMurrough— some black-haired lass with an outlandish Irish name that sounds like Eva."

"You oppose the marriage?"

He shrugged. "I don't much care what trollop Richard weds and beds. But I do care about his pretension to being a king. Ireland is a province of the English Crown, as you know. I have summoned Strongbow to come before me and explain his actions."

"Do you think he will come?" I rubbed Henry's shoulders, kneading the tight, bunched muscles

"He drags his feet; he knows he is in the wrong. But I have threatened his lands with confiscation if he does not. He likes his lands. He will come...and soon."

"I pray he sees the error of his ways and will work with you." I frowned, biting my lip in consternation when Henry could not see. I was afraid the King might decide to go on a military campaign in Ireland if he could not come to an agreement with Strongbow. That concerned me. He was not as young as he once was and I feared for him in battle; besides that, his mother Empress Maude had said Ireland was not worth the effort—the people were too wild and warlike and would never kneel to the Crown. But when had Henry truly ever listened, especially to a woman—even a woman as clever and as martial as his mother?

"I will make him. Fear not." Henry's brow was like thunder.

Strongbow came to court, the black-haired Irish bride with her strange name—Aoife—in tow, wearing her outlandish native dress. De Clare's relationship with Henry had always been cordial until now and he was eager to restore that amity. He promised that he did not intend to set himself up as any kind of Irish rival to Henry, and between them, they devised a plan of war that would bring the Irish chieftains to heel. Five thousand men at arms and five hundred powerful knights were to be sent overseas in four hundred sturdy ships.

Sick fear gripped me when I heard the news of the intended invasion, but Henry seemed glad to be off on campaign again, with Richard de Clare back in the fold and with similar aims to his own.

Soon the two men were on their way, sailing from Milford Haven with their forces. Men reported that the stormy Irish Sea was black with ships. Far away from the seashore, locked within my sturdy Tower where the winds sang, I dreamed that Henry's invasion fleet must have looked almost like the thousand ships sent to the battle of Troy. But here the jewel, the prize, was not Fair Helen but a country green as the emerald I wore on my finger—Ireland.

Little resistance met the English army when it landed; Henry was too powerful, his martial skills well known. The Irish swiftly realised only bloodshed would result from an armed encounter. In triumph, the King rode from the landing point at Waterford to the town of Dublin, where before a vast crowd of onlookers he assumed the title of 'King of Hibernia.' Richard de Clare took on the mantle of Justiciar, while other high nobles were given lordships and many lands.

In the following spring, Henry returned to England and to me. Amidst nodding daffodils and budding trees, we walked hand and hand in the Bower. Above us, the sky was a clear deep blue, promising future days of settled bliss.

"My mind is at last fully settled," he told me. "I will go to the Pope and admit I foolishly cried out for Becket's death in anger, but at the same time will plead my innocence and lack of intent regarding the deed. Then I will see my eldest son, the Young King, crowned again. In Winchester, this time."

"Crowned again?" My brows lifted in surprise.

He nodded. "Too much controversy over the Archbishop of York officiating at the first ceremony. Many consider the whole ceremony invalid. A second Coronation would appease the French King in regards to his daughter Margaret. We will crown the girl with her husband this time, and keep the moaning troublemaker quiet."

"I should like to see Winchester, my dearest."

Henry's shoulders tensed. "Rosamund, you know I do not like it when you are away from the Bower. And now that Eleanor and I are estranged, her spies may be even keener to look for the reasons why we parted in order to eliminate them. The Queen realises her position has grown precarious now that our marriage bed is cold."

"She won't be there at Winchester, will she? She is in France."

"Yes, but her spies will be lurking all over England, have no doubt of that. She likes to stay informed. Young Henry is in her pocket, too; she positively encourages him in his love of tournaments, pageants and other such claptrap. Part of her 'Courts of Love' nonsense."

"Ah yes, where people who are not married lust for each other's embrace."

Henry smiled crookedly. "Well, I suppose I can agree with that. How I do desire you, Rosamund Clifford, sinful though it may be."

"Ah," I said, eyes twinkling mischievously. "But in the Courts of Love, the two lovers must only pine for each other and never know carnal embrace! To give in to temptation would show that the love was not great enough, for all true lovers must suffer!"

"Pah! I knew the Courts of Love was a pile of horse dung!" Henry grabbed me by the waist, whirled me around, and deposited me into the shadow of the topiary. A huge green horse towered over us, leafy legs kicking the air; other branches, artfully cut, clearly showed it was meant to be a stallion. A rampant one. "I don't believe in suffering, my rose...Do you?"

"I only believe in love," I whispered, as he pressed me into the hedge, my heavy cloak forming a blanket beneath us. My arms encircled his neck; his hot breath burned my cheek. "The world is too full of suffering…But I can come to Winchester, can't I, Henry?"

"Ah, you devious minx, you have me where you want me," he laughed, as he lay down upon me in the greenery. "How could I deny you anything at this instant? You can come."

So I set out for the Young King's second Coronation, taking Blanche with me as my companion again. After our inauspicious start, we had become good friends. This time, we did not watch the grand procession into the cathedral, where the King's great uncle, the wicked William Rufus, rested in a simple tomb chest. Some said that Henry's grandsire, Henry One, had devised Rufus's death in the New Forest; Henry certainly had been riding around nearby and galloped to Winchester to declare himself King the moment the word of his brother's demise reached his ears. I would not dare to speculate; whatever had happened, it was for the best since Rufus was a hated King with unnatural vices.

Instead of attending the ceremony at the cathedral, we garnered invitations to the great banquet at the Bishop's Palace. Dressed in our finest gowns and jewels, we tried to be innocuous and self-contained, while swivel-eyed courtiers and lecherous knights side-eyed us, musing upon our identities and wondering if we were ripe for bedding. Naturally, in our disguised state, we were seated far from the high table, and some of the more bold fellows sidled up to us, trying to engage us in conversation and find out our names.

One lanky nobleman, gap-toothed and with long greasy fair hair, bowed before me. I had never met him before but recognised his device as that of Miles de Cogan, a minor lord from Glamorgan, who was now finding favour with Strongbow in Ireland.

"My greetings, milady," he said, hovering over my extended hand. I noted his hands and feet were very large and yet his limbs rather spindly, like the legs of a spider. The thought almost made me laugh in his face; I pretend to cough to hide a giggle. Blanche nudged me. "If you take no offence in my saying so, I deem you to be of beauty beyond compare. How is it that you have not been seen at court before? I could not have missed your presence; the image of your loveliness would have burned itself into my mind for all time. Do tell me, I beg you…your name."

Blanche sniffed, pushing herself in front of me. "No offence, my lord, but this is the Lady Deguise, the Lady in Disguise. She does not give out her name to strangers, even those who speak pretty words. She is not some…strumpet. Let it be known she has very good breeding."

Miles de Cogan looked startled at Blanche's forthrightness and backed away from the trestle table, face flaming with embarrassment. Then he laughed and bowed again. "I beg forgiveness, Lady 'Deguise'," he said. "I hope I have not upset you…or your little maid. I can see you wish to dine in peace; I will not disturb you again. But if, when the dancing begins, you reconsider…"

He moved away and soon vanished in the press of servers, pantlers, stewards, bright-capped fools, dancing dwarfs, nimble-limbed saltatrixes, fire breathers and other entertainers attending the banquet.

"Don't pay that Cogan fellow any attention, Lady Rosamund," said Blanche, tucking into some frumenty and sugared plums. "Not only is he ugly, he's married. Christiana, her name is. I keep abreast of such things."

I had no interest in the now-vanished de Cogan or his marital state. Indeed, unlike Blanche, I could not even muster much interest in the food, as spectacular as it was—peacocks with the feathers still attached, bright as jewels; swans with gilded beaks, gliding on gilt trays; even a great fat porpoise dragged from the Norfolk coast that wallowed in briny sauce.

I was more concerned with what was happening at the high table, where the Young King sat in splendour beneath a gold canopy, his listless young bride Margaret sitting behind him, pouting as she poked at her trencher. Henry was standing near his son's seat, his expression rather hot and furious; I knew immediately that there was ill feeling between father and son.

My gaze flicked to the Young King; effete and indolent, his silk-shod feet rested on a stool, while a gaggle of sweating, nervous pages and squires milled around him to meet his every whim. He was now seventeen, a man, and had grown in height and breadth since I had first seen him at the illegal Westminster Coronation. His long red-gold hair fell to his shoulders and his jaw was firm, his demeanour both spoilt and imperious. As wicked as it was, and despite that he was my lover's trueborn son, I found myself disliking the youth. I no longer saw him as the lost possibility of a son. Now I saw less in him of Henry and more of his mother, Eleanor—I was sure the arrogant tilt of his head and the slightly smug smile on the almost-pretty lips were inherited from her.

I wanted desperately to find out what had happened. As the music from the minstrels swelled up and a courtly dance began, I leapt from my bench while Blanche stared open-mouthed and grabbed myself a handsome lordling (Miles de Cogan was nowhere in sight, thank goodness). The young man, some years my junior, looked nearly as flabbergasted as my lady-in-waiting, but rather pleased when I jabbered at him that I desired to dance to the honour of the newly crowned King. Taking my arm, he swept me out amidst the crowd of dancers. By a combination of luck and device, I managed to dance up close to the high table just as the Young King was rising from his seat. Henry was beckoning him to follow him from the banqueting chamber; my lover was flushed with anger, while Young Henry looked perturbed and flustered.

"Ah, so sorry, you must excuse me." I tried to affect an air of great sorrow towards my dancer partner. "I must run, alas. Too much wine, sir, if you understand my meaning."

The young knight blushed like an affronted maiden, and I lifted up my heavy skirts and hurried in the direction the King and his son had taken. If questioned by anyone, I decided I would play the innocent and claim I was merely seeking the palace garderobes.

Luckily, as I entered the corridor leading from the banqueting hall, I heard raised voices and ducked into an embrasure, attempting to make myself small and invisible. The torches had burned low; shadows fluttered round me like a cloak.

Near at hand, I heard Henry's angry roar and the petulant whine as the Young King responded.

"No, Hell, a thousand times, no. How often do you have to be told, boy?"

"Don't call me boy, father. Someone might hear. It is undignified. I am not a boy. I am a King."

"In name only. As you well know."

"I still must live as a King; otherwise the people will mock me." Young Henry's tone grew even more petulant. "As it is, the income granted me does not cover my basic expenses. My robes, my wife's wardrobe, my horses, tapestries for the walls, decent wine for my companions…I need money for these!"

"You're only destitute because you spend too bloody much time involved in tournaments. Riding around jabbing at your friends with lances. You know I disapprove of it and even forbade it here in

England, but still you insist on competing—spending coin you do not possess to hold your Godless tourneys in the Low Countries instead."

"You are trying to squeeze out all of life's joy!" cried the Young King dramatically. "You grow old and clearly do not see the honour and glory that is the tournament."

"Oh, do shut up, *boy.* Cut down on your frivolity, Henry, I am warning you. Only when you show some sense, will I cede any more power to you…or increase your income."

"That is not fair!" I gritted my teeth at the Young King's strident whine. "Why do you hate me so, father? You have done better for my other brother, Richard! Look at him, riding around Aquitaine as if he were a king—when I am a King, not him. Richard is laughing at me!"

"Everyone is laughing at you. You are feckless. How did Eleanor and I ever produce such a simpleton? You're as thick as pig's swill, Henry!"

"How dare you!"

"I dare. Believe me, I dare. You have been too longer under your mother's influence. You will bend knee to me, your sire, while I live."

"Well, if you dare to be offensive to your firstborn, then I shall dare to be offensive to a sour old greybeard of a father," said Young Henry, sounding like a three-year-old child in a rage, having been denied a pony ride or his favourite wooden sword. "I am going to make my court brighter and more entertaining than yours ever was, just to spite you. How about…" the Young King was clearly mocking his father now and clearly drunk, too, "how about, I hold a lavish banquet where every man attending must be called 'William' after the Conqueror? What do you think of that? Amusing sport, I'd say."

"I'd say you were a fool. You great lump…you'd be shutting yourself out of your own damned banquet!"

There was a strangled noise from the Young King as he realised his mockery had fallen flat and *he* was being mocked instead. "Enough of this talk, father! I have no wish to further discuss with you what I do in my own time, within my own court. I just want my inheritance."

"You will get it when I deem you sensible enough not to waste it. Kingship is more than a constant round of hunting, drinking and whoring."

"Well, you've done enough of the latter!" sniped Young Henry.

I choked at that and pressed my hand to my mouth to muffle the noise. Unexpectedly, my eyes began to tear. The embrasure where I hid was thick with the summer's dust; the servants had clearly not cleaned the corridor well before the Coronation. I could not stop myself; suddenly I emitted a loud sneeze that rang throughout the passage.

A moment's silence reigned. I held my breath, hoping against hope. Then a long, lean, wiry arm clad in cloth of gold reached into the niche and grabbed hold of my arm, dragging me from my hiding spot. Horrified, I stared up into the handsome, arrogant, elegant face of Henry the Young King. The freckles on his nose stood out like specks of paint as his visage whitened with wrath. "Who are you? And why, by Christ's Nails, were you eavesdropping on me and my father?"

"My lord King." I sagged in his grip; he let me fall and I crashed painfully to my knees with my head bowed. "I meant no disrespect. I...I heard voices, and when I realised who it was, I was too afraid to either press forward or go back to the hall, so I hid."

"A likely tale." Young Henry's eyes narrowed. "I trust no one, least of all a wench flitting around in the dark. A woman can wield a knife as easily as a man and is more likely to hide a weapon rather than engage in honest fight. Where do you have the weapon hidden, woman? " A new light entered his eyes and it was an unpleasant one. "You're rather pretty, aren't you?" He pulled me towards him.

"Unhand her. She is with me." Knocking his son's hot hands away, Henry thrust himself in front of the Young King, a stalwart barrier of muscle and resolve. "She's one of mine."

"Oh." Backing off abruptly, the Young King wiped his hands on his ermine robes as if he had just touched something dirty. "One of your whores. You dare to lecture me on behaviour yet you bring a whore to my Coronation? You are such a hypocrite, father." He peered at me critically from under his fair, feathery brows. An angel's face but one of the Devil's Brood. I noted his eyes were the same mixed colour as Henry's but nowhere near so shrewd...and not in the least intelligent. "Comely, though. I would not mind throwing a few coins in her direction if you are inclined to share. Margaret is a fine wife, but she...she is in her woman's time. What's the trull called?"

"I am sure you have heard of her." Henry said, planting his hands on his hips. He was like a huge oak, strong and imposing, while the Young King was but a weedy sapling, bending in the wind. "Her name..." He paused as if deliberating whether he should speak or not.

I held my breath. Was he, at last, going to divulge my identity? To Eleanor's son, of all men? Someone who had every reason to hate me, the thief of what should have been reserved for his mother?

"Her name is...BelleBelle."

Young Henry's nose wrinkled as if he smelt something sour and I began to cough again, covering both a gasp and a surge of unexpected laughter. "Oh, yes, that infamous trollop! The one renowned for her special...*dancing*. And her enormous..." The Young King made a cupping motion at his chest.

"Yes, that one."

"I have heard half the court has joined in her 'entertainments' at one time or another. Was she not said to have once used a snake...?"

"She is a warm, loving, experienced girl. She likes to share. As for the snake...she is an actor, she was portraying Eve."

"Not for me such an overblown harlot, playing lewd games with serpents. Eve, indeed." Face screwed up in disgust, young Henry scooped up his trailing robes. "Keep her to yourself, father. I have no wish to risk catching a pox."

Henry shrugged. "So be it. I wasn't offering and neither was the lady. Do you have any more to say to me, or are you just going to stand here and insult my leman?"

"I have said enough. Just remember, I want my inheritance, father, and I will get it one way or another! Now I bid you farewell. Enjoy your whore."

Young Henry stalked away into the gloom, leaving me alone with the King. He was staring at me, his gaze as angry and accusatory as his son's had been. "What was in your bloody mind, Rosamund?" he snarled. "That was dangerous."

"I needed the privy." I told him my lie. "Everything I said was true."

His lips thinned to lines and I was sure he knew I was uttering a falsehood, then his mood abruptly lightened and he began to laugh. "Well, if nothing more, you have seen what I have to deal with in my family. Constant strife, constant insolence, constant aggravation. Fuelled by Eleanor, of course. Johnny is the only one who loves me. Only him. And he's just a little boy; God knows what kind of man he'll become."

"You think your Henry could be a danger to you? Or even Richard and Geoffrey?"

"Aye." He nodded gravely. "I don't trust any of them. But let's not talk of that. If Young Henry thinks I am busy with a harlot...Well, let us go to my apartments and make busy. I would rather look at you than at his pugnacious little face."

"I don't know," I teased. "While I understand that you might wish to hide my identity, why of all your paramours did you claim I was BelleBelle? The one with the enormous…"

"Heart…" he finished wryly. "Well, I knew Young Henry can be a bit …over-fastidious and pernickety where women are concerned. He caught something once. Nasty. He wouldn't insist on sampling the wares if he thought they'd been sampled too many times before."

I shuddered, imagining if father and son had come to blows over possessing my body. Henry's hand curled over mine, strong, implacable, drawing me forward into the safety of his arms. "The night is growing old; let us not waste what is left of it. Damn the rest of the banquet; Henry will not miss us. Come on, I burn for you…BelleBelle."

I allowed myself to laugh. But I did not want to think overmuch about mistress BelleBelle and her serpent.

I was back at Woodstock. Henry was overseas, dealing with his sons. His letters came fast and furious this time, keeping me informed of what was happening abroad. The Young King was in high dudgeon because Henry had awarded his younger brother John three Norman castles, Mirabeau, Chinon and Loudun, and arranged a match for him with Alixe, daughter of Humbert of Maurienne. The castles had belonged to Young Henry and he was in no mood to give them away. However, his father's will was paramount, and so the fortresses were duly handed over to the child John, and with sour and glowering ill will the Young King signed and sealed the marriage treaty for his brother.

It is madness, dear flower, Henry wrote to me. *I have tried everything. I have even restricted the size of Henry's entourage so that he will live within his means. I have weeded out his less savoury friends who press him to rise against me, but my efforts to keep control have come to naught. I persuaded Eleanor and Richard to fare to Poitiers, while I took Henry to Chinon, where I hoped, free of her influence, we might learn to be friends again. He threw tantrums like a child and I made him stay in my chamber all night that I might watch him…but by the Rood, the moment I grew weary and my eyes closed, he was out the door haring his way towards Paris. King Louis sheltered him, naturally, ever eager to cause trouble…but here is the part that grieves me most, beloved. Richard and Geoffrey have sided with their errant brother. This means, my Rose of the World, that there will be war. And it will surely spread to England, for my son's supporters believe he is more fit to rule there than I. William Marshall stands beside him and he is a mighty warrior. May God keep you. Pray for me. Burn this letter, as ever. H. R.*

Unfortunately, Henry's unhappy predictions soon came true. Rumours spread of unrest in the northlands and across the Middle shires. Robert de Beaumont, Earl of Leicester, gathered a pack of Flemish mercenaries and sailed from Normandy to join Hugh Bigod of Norfolk and other disaffected and treasonous nobles in rebellion against their rightful lord.

The rebels met the King's forces, led by Justiciar Robert de Lucie and High Constable Humphrey de Bohun, at a ford near Bury St Edmunds. Bigod and Beaumont, both proud and ill-tempered men, had fallen to quarrelling and hence split their armies, weakening their force, and soon the Earl of Leicester's mercenaries were dispersed and driven into the swampland, where locals sprang from the reeds like bloodthirsty swamp-demons and clubbed, stabbed and pitchforked them to death. The mercenaries' corpses were weighted down and deposited in the bog.

De Beaumont and his wife Petronilla were captured after a brief fight, where to the amazement and amusement of the victors, it became clear Petronilla was wearing a man's armour beneath her cloak. The unfortunate couple were paraded around the country as examples, with wags declaring that Countess Petronilla was surely the better warrior of the two. The rebellion in the East had failed utterly.

But once a fire is kindled, it is hard to douse it again. William the Lion, King of Scots, sent his brother David of Huntingdon to attempt to take the north. Nottingham burned, torched by William de Ferrers, Earl of Derby, while Northampton's walls were assailed by siege towers and grappling hooks.

Receiving the news from Blanche's contacts and others, I was intensely fearful and so were Blanche and Orable. If Henry's forces should be defeated by some horrible mischance, what would become of us? We would be spoils of war, property of whoever desired us. Tower and Bower had been built to hide me from a jealous queen and her minions but it was not a war-castle, even though its walls were stout, and it would not withstand a protracted siege. A few blows from an iron-headed ram and the door would most likely come down.

I spent much time on my knees in prayer, with old Father Morland attempting to bring me comfort. "Go to the nuns, Lady Rosamund!" he begged, still trying to save my unchaste soul…and perhaps my frail woman's body too. But I would not go. My decision was made. I was loyal to my lover.

Battles in Brittany and Normandy and Anjou and Maine continued, reports reaching the Bower from across the stormy Channel; I could only pray to Jesu and the Blessed Virgin that Henry would prevail against his disloyal children and the barons who joined their forces. Louis of France, eager to partake of Henry's ruin was rampaging through all the various territories owned by his adversary, burning the crops and firing villages but it would seem, in his ill thought out malevolence, also destroying the main sources of food for his own armies. Motivated by the power of fury, Henry plunged after him, marching from Rouen to Dol in a single day, a feat wondered at by even the most battle-hardened soldiers, for such a trek was deemed beyond human capabilities. Yet he did it and his men followed him gladly, true knights who served their lord.

A letter arrived from Henry, brought by messengers in salt-encrusted, sodden cloaks; they had ridden like the wind from the port at Southampton. I thanked them for their services and carried the sealed scroll from my Lord into the privacy of my apartments, breaking the red wax open with shaking fingers.

It will only be a matter of time before I return to England, dearest Rosamund. My son Yong Henry is as pitiful at warfare as he is at everything else...except for drinking and hunting! His allies deserted him. I fared to Gisors to meet him at the elm tree where France and England have frequently treated for peace throughout the years, and he would have offered his submission, but God smite him dead, that fiend King Louis managed to convince Henry, Richard and Geoffrey to scorn my generous terms! So my return cannot be quite yet; negotiation must continue but I have no doubt it will be before the summer at the latest. I know this may seem long, but be of good cheer, beloved Rose, for I have good news—the Archbishop of Rouen sided with me and threatened to excommunicate Eleanor for her evil in inciting treason. She fled towards Paris dressed as a man, but I was on to her tricks and apprehended her. She is imprisoned now, Rosamund, and will remain so. Soon, there shall be no impediment to a life in public. Burn this at once, I bid you. H.R.

My head went light and my knees weak; I heaved a huge sigh of relief as I crumpled the parchment and hurled it onto the brazier as the King requested. It hissed, sizzled, fell to black ashes.

Soon. Soon I might be free of Tower and Bower...forever.

I waited. He did not come. Winter swirled round the Tower; icicles hung from the parapet edge, tinkling as they broke off and fell to the snowy ground below. Patch, an old dog now, lay by the fire in the kitchens, deaf and toothless. I savoured even a dog's companionship in my lover's long absence, but Patch had rather attached himself to Cook, who fed him many titbits, and I would not remove his aching old bones from the comfortable warmth just for my pleasure.

I heard that Henry spent Christmas with his youngest son, John. Eleanor continued to languish in prison, though I dare say she suffered not overmuch or had many privations.

Then the Young King, still stewing about perceived wrongs visited on him by his father, started the affray again—and in rage and dismay at his lack of military success in Anjou and Aquitaine, turned his attention on England, slumbering in an uneasy peace after the burning and looting of the year past. Once again, William of Scotland's troops streamed over the borders, trumpets blaring, and with little effort, the rebel forces captured Carlisle. Those great barons who had not fared abroad with the King begged Henry to return to England as quickly as he might before the rebellion spread.

By summer Henry was here, reaching the port of Dover after sailing through a great storm that raised waves as high as ships in the Channel. Bells clanged in joyous greeting and the common folk celebrated in the street. Passing through Dover town, Henry halted at the mighty castle on the cliff, the guardian of the gateway to England, where Hugh de Mara held the position of Keeper of the Coast. Having refreshed himself within those sturdy walls, he set off with his entourage for Canterbury, with the scattered remnants of Eleanor's court in tow—and Eleanor herself, under close guard, with soldiers gathered in formation around her litter, their spears bristling like the quills of the exotic porcupine in the menagerie at Woodstock.

Reaching the city of Canterbury, Eleanor and a solitary lady-in-waiting, a girl called Amaria, were sent onwards in a guarded chariot to the windy fortress of Sarum, far from any centres of rebellion. Far from Woodstock. Far from Henry.

And then Henry Plantagenet, the King returned, sent for me.

He was about to do penance, and he wanted me there.

The carriage that came to bear me to Canterbury was no longer unmarked, but bore Henry's device clearly upon its frame in gold, flaring in the sun. Rampant lions roared on the tabards of the drivers and the soldiers who rode protectively alongside, mailed and helmeted, with pennons flying overhead. Blanche and Orable journeyed with me, dressed splendidly, as the King had sent us all new gowns. Blanche's attire was a soft green, the colour of a spring leaf, while Orable's was pale blue with exquisite stitchery on the sleeves and neckline, but my dress was the most elaborate of all, wrought of silk imported from foreign eastern lands dyed a deep rose red. The sleeves were long, lined in paler silk, and blue and gold beadwork decorated cuff and neckline.

A girdle of golden wires had arrived with it and an elaborate circlet studded with rubies thick as plums.

The journey to Canterbury was uneventful and to pass the time I stared out of the window to enjoy the beauties of the countryside, basking under a hot July sun. We crossed the Weald of Kent with its myriad farms, green and fruitful, and then, exciting rising in me, I spotted Canterbury Cathedral's spire in the distance—that holy place, the site of many miracles since Thomas Becket had died. He had been canonised only recently; the fractious priest was now a saint.

We entered the town through mighty Westgate with its twin drum towers and proceeded up King's bridge, where masons were hard at work on a new building—a hospital where pilgrims could rest on their way to St Thomas's new shrine. The streets were heaving with merchants and peasants, monks and nuns in grey and white and brown, and bells clanged from the churches and abbeys—St Martin's and St Mary Magdalene's, St Mildred's and St Peter's, and wealthy St Augustine's where Christianity first was preached in England.

Near the entrance to the close, we alighted from the chariot and were escorted to a viewing platform raised near the huge doors of the cathedral. The shadows from its five towers stretched over us; saints stared down from niches in the west front, stony-eyed. Bells chimed from a freestanding campanile built on a hummock within the cathedral grounds, summoning people to come, see a King abased, a King punished, a King expiating his guilt.

The crowd thickened, pressing inwards toward the cathedral, a sea of faces—rich men, paupers, goodwives, the religious. Guards pushed them back with the butts of their spears, forcing a passageway through the crowded close to the cathedral steps. The same guards also ringed the platform where I stood with Orable, Blanche, and other women of noble blood, protecting us from any sudden violence or rioting.

I began to sweat and was glad a cloth canopy fluttered over us to shield us from the relentless July sun. The stench of the crowds, mixed with the odour of animals and the rancid gutters in the streets beyond, curled up to choke my lungs.

Henry…and where was Henry? Tension crackled in the air like summer's lightning, and I could sense a vague air of hostility in the gathered mob. Not all were willing to accept the King's submission to the Church and absolve him of the stain of murder. Becket had been popular in Canterbury, much more so than the King.

A horn sounded a fanfare, its clear call cutting through the clangour of the bells in the campanile. The crowd roared and milled for a moment, then fell into a deep, unnatural silence. It was eerie, as if God Himself has smitten the onlookers dumb, wresting their tongues away. Abruptly the bells ceased to chime, both at the cathedral and across the whole of Canterbury, and the campanile rang out single great booms, deep as drumbeats.

A solitary child cried out, voice rising in a wail of fear that was cut off as its mother jammed her hand across its open mouth.

Into the close walked Henry, flanked by two knights and by esteemed and ancient men of the Church, stern-visaged, the sun shining off shaven pates and glinting on white beards. The King was barefoot and his feet were bleeding from his long, unshod journey from St Dunstan's church on the edge of Canterbury. Bloody footprints smeared the flagstones behind him, glistening sickeningly in the sunlight. Gone were his kingly robes, replaced by a penitent's garment of humble sackcloth. Ash smeared his face as further evidence of his newfound humility.

Moving slowly, shoulders bowed, he shuffled to the steps leading up to the cathedral door. He was taken in, guided by a contingent of monks; I knew he was being taken to the crypt where Becket's sword-mutilated bones lay buried, where he would prostrate himself and beg God for forgiveness in his part in the murder.

But he would return. Henry's ultimate punishment was to be public, before the eyes of all men.

After what seemed an eternity, during which I felt faint and Blanche fanned my face, and the hordes of watchers grew restive, Henry appeared in the cathedral doorway, a dark, stumbling figured limned by the light of the hundreds of candles burning within the vestibule.

Silence fell again.

Moving stiffly, as if he were a very ancient man, he knelt on the steps, back to the watching crowd, bowing his head as low as was possible, until his brow nearly touched the stonework. Then the monks filed out of the cloister, their faces white as death and their tonsured heads beaded with sweat, and in their hands they bore new-cut branches covered in spiky fronds.

A bishop in tall mitre went to the King's side and divested him of his upper raiment. His bare back, scarred from battles long past, gleamed in the sun. I knew each of those scars, loved every one. I could hardly bear to look.

"In the name of God," the bishop cried, his crow-harsh voice echoing between the towers and the walls of the houses in the close, "we punish this man, this King, who through his unrighteous wrath and loose tongue brought about the death of St Thomas, now blessed and sanctified, and polluted the sanctity of God's House with unlawful bloodshed. Let him be flogged here as any common criminal might be punished…but then let him be fully absolved of his sin, for he will have duly done penance for his crime as prescribed by the Holy Father in Rome."

The bishop took a branch from one of the monks and raised it on high. Then he brought it down with a crack across Henry's exposed back, shattering the branch in twain with the force of his blow. The King did not flinch. The Bishop picked up one half of the branch and struck again, again, again and again, until the tree-limb fell into many pieces, which he flung contemptuously down upon the steps.

Four more Bishops took over, continuing to administer Henry's penance with almost unseemly gusto. Five times each they flogged him with the thorny tree branches before snapping the boughs in half and casting them aside.

No sooner were they done than the assembled monks surged forth and whipped Henry too, striking him three times each. All through the first beatings, the King remained silent but now he began to wince with each new blow. Bruising glowed dark along the ridge of his spine and the skin weltered thin streaks of blood. One hundred holy men lashed him three hundred times for his involvement in Thomas Becket's death.

By the final strokes of punishment, I was flinching even as the King flinched. Bile stung my mouth and tears streamed down my cheeks. I was sure many wondered why I wept—perhaps they thought it was for poor, murdered Becket—but I no longer cared what others thought.

Near to me, out of the corner of my tearing eye, I saw a man in the crowd, sunburnt and sneering, lifting up a ragged child to witness the King's humiliation. "Lookit that, James. Did ye ever think you'd see such a wonder? A King bein' struck, just like a peasant. And look you, lad…'e's bleedin red blood just like the rest of us! Lookit all that bleedin' blood!"

I looked, my stomach twisted, suddenly my ears rang, and the bright day darkened as if a storm were leaping in my head and in my eyes. Silently, I slumped down into the arms of Orable and Blanche and remembered little more.

The sky was red outside the window, bunched clouds dripping sunrise's glorious colour. I turned on my side, blinking in the incarnadine light. Birds were chirping in the trees in an unseen garden, singing a hymn to the glory of the ascending sun.

After I fainted at the cathedral, I had been borne out of the town of Canterbury to Westenhanger Castle near Folkestone. Despite his own injuries, the King had ordered it, placing my welfare above his own. Weak and with pounding head, I was carried into the castle on a litter and placed in a bed with stern-looking physicians all around me. Too much sun, they declared. Too much heat. Too much emotion. They had given me wine and medicinal drinks, and I slept under Blanche and Orable's watchful gaze.

I did not know how long I slept, only that the draughts given me by the physicians gave me strange, haunting dreams.

A hand descended on my shoulder, stroking its tip through my thin chemise. A loving caress, calling me back to the world. Dream or reality? Breath rushed between my clenched teeth. Rolling over onto my back, I stared up into the visage of my lover, the King.

I struggled to sit, and then to climb from the bed. "My lord…Henry!" I cried, and I burst into tears and flung my arms around him.

"Steady, steady, Rosamund," he said, half-laughing, though I could hear the pain in his voice. "Be careful where you put those fair white hands; I am a little sore."

"I saw it all," I wept. "Your poor back…your poor feet. I would gladly wash and anoint your wounds like Luke tells us a sinful woman did to Christ: *And she stood at his feet behind him weeping, and began to wash his feet with tears, and did wipe them with the hairs of her head, and kissed his feet, and anointed them with the ointment.*"

"Ah, my dear, sweet Rosamund," Henry said. "I would not have you wipe that beautiful russet hair upon soles that have endured the muck of Canterbury streets. I will heal…and truth be told, I deserved all those blows, every one. But I must put the events in Canterbury behind me and look forward to the running of my kingdoms. The debt has been paid, amends made to God and man. Thomas, I believe has forgiven me my sins against him; there has been a sign."

"A sign? What sign?"

Henry's mouth curved in a broad grin, showing straight white teeth. "Tidings have reached me from the north. Ranulph de Glanville has taken William the Lion prisoner at Alnwick. The Scots King was besieging the castle but had left himself rather short of men—his bodyguards amounted to a mere sixty. Glanville attacked at dawn and took him captive when William's horse was killed beneath him. The Lion now lies imprisoned within the walls of Newcastle. The rebels in England are fleeing and the Scots have retreated; while there still may be trouble in France, it is over here. Over."

"I am glad," I whispered.

Henry placed his hand beneath my chin, tilting my head up. "I will send your women to tend you. Dress and come down to the hall. We will dine."

And so I entered the hall, in my red gown, and the lords of the land stopped to stare at this strange woman whose name they did not know. Blushing, I halted and cast down my eyes, but Henry rose from his seat upon the dais, and moving stiffly after his beating, he approached me and took my hand in his, leading me to a seat set up beneath his canopy of state. An audible gasp rippled through the throng; some looked disapproving while others jabbered in excitement behind their hands.

The King glanced around the hall, eyes burning with passion, as if daring anyone present to speak out against me. "This is Rosamund de Clifford, daughter of Walter," he said, his voice rising clear as a church bell above the mutter of voices.

It was all he said.

It was all he needed to say.

So the secret was out…but after a few days in Westenhanger, followed by several more in London, where I lived almost as a Queen in the Palace of Westminster, I was taken back to Woodstock and the Bower. Henry travelled with me to stay for a few days.

"I thought my seclusion might be over." I tried not to show my disappointment as we trailed around the labyrinth. "That we are lovers is known to all men, and Eleanor is imprisoned. What harm can she bring me now, locked away with her maid in Sarum?"

Henry's expression was serious. "Believe it or not, dear-heart, she still has friends; more than one might think. She was a very influential woman and could be...mesmerising. You must realise that. The danger to you *may* have abated...or it may have increased, at least for a little while."

"What do you mean?"

Henry sighed, folding his arms over his broad chest. "When I still lived with Eleanor, you would have been seen as yet another mistress, one of many. But with Eleanor put away...men are talking. They guess what is in my mind in regards to you—that I seek an annulment of my marriage so I can wed you instead. Such news causes Eleanor to writhe in rage like an angry dragon or so my spies report. I have offered her freedom if she should take the veil and enter Fontevraud Abbey...but she has refused me. She will be a thorn in my side as long as she can, I fear. And part of being such a thorn will be to assail all I hold dear."

"What about consanguinity? Did you not tell me you are kin within the prohibited degrees? What about an appeal to the Pope?"

"It is true that Eleanor and I are related but because we clearly knew this when we wed makes the granting of an annulment on those grounds less likely. If I could prove my father Geoffrey lay with the bitch, that might go in my favour, but Eleanor claims that rumours of that union are lies and that she drove my father from her chamber door with many rebukes. He told me face to face that he swived her many times and recommended her to me because she was rampant between the sheets! But whether my story will be believed over hers, I do not know. It is a difficult charge to prove."

I hung my head. "I will abide here in the Bower till the matter is dealt with, then."

"You are a good girl." He kissed my lips with passion.

Feeling unusually peevish, I moved my head away from his, ending the kiss abruptly. "I am not a girl any longer, Henry. I am in the latter part of my twenties...and have no true husband and no children."

Henry gazed upon me in silence. I stared back, wondering if I had sparked one of his infamous rages. Instead, he placed his hands on my shoulders. "Just a little more patience, my Rose of the World. In due time, you will be raised to a wife's estate and when we are together night after night, and bound in legal wedlock, I have no doubt we will have a brood as large as my family by Eleanor!"

Soon after Henry left Woodstock, hastening for France where his sons were still stirring up trouble, and I was left thinking…If Henry *did* put aside Eleanor to marry me and I produced children, how would those rebellious sons of his take the news? The Young King resented even giving a solitary castle to his landless youngest brother. How would he feel about children of his mother's supplanter, especially as they would be born in wedlock? And, even more frightening, if the King's marriage was annulled using Geoffrey's carnal knowledge of Eleanor as a reason, could it come about that all her children be declared illegitimate or disinherited? The marriage would be thought incestuous; could one huge step lead to another? And if Henry's children were removed from the succession, that would make any children of mine….

Cheeks burning, conflicted, I pressed my hands to my face. I dared not think about it. Could not, lest I go mad and drown myself in the well that bore my name.

The rebellion of the young Eaglets, the dissatisfied sons of Henry Two, was truly over. The Young King's revenues had been slashed, impeding his ability to make war, while Richard had lost several castles. This younger, most martial son of my lover had seemed most distraught as he recognised his own folly and had thrown himself at his father's feet, weeping as he begged forgiveness for his crimes.

Once reconciliation had taken place, I had hoped Henry would be able to spend more time with me, but he was like the wind, ever moving, ever sweeping on to new destinations. In Valogne he received homage from the captive William of Scotland and forced him to sign a treaty that would keep the Scots in subjugation and disable their most powerful border fortresses. At the same time, he arranged for his illegitimate half-sister Emma, one of Geoffrey Plantagenet's byblows, to wed Davydd, a Welsh prince, in hopes that such a union would bind England and Wales together and foster peace.

It was July next year before we saw each other again. Henry's entourage had come to Woodstock Palace, where, with the Young King, he was to rest a while before continuing to Gloucester, where he planned to meet with the cream of the Welsh nobility. It was to be a grand spectacle, with William of Scotland parading around on a grey charger while the Young King lorded it over him, dressed in cloth of gold and riding on a milk-white steed. The symbolism was, of course, clear…and meant to impress, of subtly threaten, the Welsh princes, who were there to swear allegiance to Henry's heir.

"I would take you to Gloucester, my dearest, now that men know of us," said Henry apologetically, "but I still fear the Queen may have evil planned, and with her son being there, I would not risk it. I would have no time to see to your well-being, and it would lie heavy on my mind. Gerald de Barri, the Archdeacon of Brecknock will be there too, with the Welsh contingent, and he…"

"And he is an odious, unpleasant little man who acts well above his station!" I retorted hotly. "To say nothing of the fact he seems overly concerned with who is bedding whom. Did he not report his predecessor's supposed adultery and get the man removed from his position? He has done nicely for himself out of passing on tittle-tattle, I hear, living as he does off countless tithes of wood and cheese. He seems an idle layabout; spends more time writing scurrilous accounts of what others are doing than tending to his flock."

Henry roared with laughter; I felt less amused. Gerald of Wales, upon learning of my liaison with the King, had supposedly said of me that I was 'not Rosamund but *rosa immunda*, the unclean rose...not the Rose of the World, but *rosa immundi*, the rose of filth or unchastity'.

"Why do you laugh?" I said with sullen bad humour. "Some would think he deserves punishment for such harsh and unfair words."

"One day he will be silenced." Henry chucked me under the chin. "When you are raised to the highest estate in the land."

"How is Eleanor?" My voice was flat, stony.

"Still in Sarum. She complained it was cold and I let her stay in Winchester awhile…under strict guard, naturally. Now that it's summer, she's back to Sarum."

"Any news on the annulment? Surely she grows sick of the long years of her imprisonment."

"No." Henry's face grew shuttered. "She will not countenance it under any circumstances, she says…unless she retains Aquitaine."

"And you will not give up Aquitaine yourself. For anything on this earth."

"I have made my son Richard Duke there! I would not see him lose such an important territory."

"Maybe it would not be lost. Maybe Eleanor would be glad to let it go to Richard after her own demise. After all, Richard is her son as well as yours, and her favourite, I've heard. It is only you that she has grown to hate."

A muscle jumped in Henry's stern jaw; his eyes became the hue of storm clouds. "I will not cede Aquitaine. Eleanor will pay for her treason and she will continue in captivity until she gives me what I desire—the lands and my bloody freedom!"

I huddled down, despondent. We were in the labyrinth, the odd, uncouth topiary shapes, now somewhat overgrown and neglected, towering over us. *The accursed lands of Aquitaine!* Would they at the end prove more important to Henry than our union?"

"I must go now," said the King, rising suddenly from the marble seat upon which he had sat, legs stretched out before him. "There is much to arrange. Do not look so sad, Rosamund; it cannot be long before Eleanor breaks. Once she is veiled or gone to France or gone to the devil, we will be together, I swear by the True Cross, by everything that is holy. Eleanor's court was called the Court of Love, but it will be nothing akin to ours when the time comes."

"I must learn to have more faith, Henry," I said, and kissed him with ardour to show that I had not become peevish, for it would do me no good to drive a wedge between us.

He smiled down at me, slipped his arms around me, and squeezed my slender waist until I felt that I should snap like a twig. "Not much longer, Rosamund. I promise you."

Henry went upon his way, wrapped in the business of Kings. But this time he left something with me. Within a few weeks I began to spew in the mornings, unable to even hold down sops, and then I realised my courses had ceased.

I was with child.

It seemed a miracle after so long, though the amount of time I spent apart from the King was not conducive to pregnancy. Yet here I was, only a few years off thirty summers, bearing my first child, a royal bastard.

Blanche treated me as if I would break, ordering the kitchens to prepare the finest delicacies. I wrote to Henry to break the news, hoping he might come galloping back to Woodstock, but he did not. He was far too busy with matters of state. That is not to say he was not joyous at the coming birth of our child, far from it; he sent a wooden cradle, skilfully carved, and fine bedclothes stitched with the Royal Arms, and promised to have candles burnt for a safe delivery at shrines across England.

The birth of another son shall be a great joy, he wrote to me. *I know it will be a boy, I feel it deep within; a loyal son, unlike those given me by Eleanor...save for dear young Johnny, too youthful to rebel! I want you to name him William, Rosamund. This, after so many years, is a sign from God, I am certain. Christ willing, Eleanor's stiff back will soon break, and we will be free of her malign influence. But as you know, the deed must be done with care; she says she will not take the veil and if an annulment was granted and she should choose remarriage instead of the Church, she might well wed some powerful king who would make war against me. I know you will understand, my Rose of the World, as patient as the Greek Penelope...*

I sighed and tossed his letter into the fire, as I had agreed always to do to protect our privacy. *William.* I touched my belly lightly. William had been the name of the first child of Henry and Eleanor; the little boy who died of a seizure at Wallingford Castle, aged just three, and was buried at his grandfather's feet in Reading Abbey. A tiny sword had been wrought for him and taken to lie on the altar in Jerusalem in his memory.

William. Henry's firstborn and now our firstborn, should it be a boy. And it would be. I felt it as strongly as Henry did.

William.

I stood within the labyrinth. The November sky above was a tableau of grey. Shrieking from the North East, the wind scored my face, tossed my unbound hair. Here, in seclusion, I could wear it loose like a maiden still. Once Eleanor was gone and I came to court, no more.

I sighed. A bare tree bough, black and bony as a skeleton's claw, caught at my arm. It was daggered by tiny icicles that dripped as the day warmed up almost imperceptibly. Drip, drip, drip. Ten drips of water like cold tears; one for each of the ten years I had dwelt in the Tower at Woodstock.

Ten years.

My mood was dark, my spirits low; a cavalcade of new fears seized me. Half the time, I wished to escape, to flee back to Clifford Castle to be with my mother Margaret when the child was born. But mother was ailing and often bedridden, and I had no wish to see my father, by all reports as violent and hard as ever. The other half of me wanted nothing more than to stay here, in my cocoon, a butterfly never opening its wings to the world, protected by thick walls, by locked doors, by a thorny maze.

I would be...*safe.* My baby would be safe. Protectively I cradled my growing belly.

Henry had told me of my safety in the Bower, repeatedly he had told me....

The days grew darker as November marched into December. Tallow candles burned, their sweet scent permeating the Tower. I watched the sun blaze down to its wintry death from my turret room and hoped Henry might be free of his troubles and toils and seek my company. He did not but the gifts came, silks and brocade and a Christening gown of highest quality for the babe. He would not forget me. I told myself that, and yet, as my body bloomed, I was full of doubts and fears in a way I had not been for years. The midwife who Blanche brought from the nearby village of Bladon confirmed that such troubled thoughts frequently afflicted breeding women, and I was to rest my mind.

But my mind did not rest.

Feverish, I wrote my will, as did all sensible women who were with child. Childbirth was dangerous, one of our punishments through Eve. Many died, and the baby with them. Perhaps God would punish me for fornication, for adultery…but Henry thought my pregnancy was a sign of God's approval. A sign that the detestable Eleanor would no longer hold sway over us…

I thought of Eleanor, ancient now and bitter-eyed, celibate as a nun, incapable of charming kings and Saracen lords and troubadours. Locked in Sarum where, 'twas said, the wind never stopped shrieking over the mighty earth ramparts, where the solitary entrance was over a long bridge spanning a deep moat filled with wooden spikes to deter invaders. And I thought…was she really so unlike me, except that I was still loved? We were both confined, unable to leave our places of isolated confinement…and Henry Plantagenet was master of our fates.

While I ruminated darkly on my life, I had failed to notice that the food coming out of the kitchen was of poorer quality than usual, and less of it. My maid Blanche was the one who pointed it out to me. "I am so sorry, Lady Rosamund," she said, as she handed me a silver tray with a solitary little fish upon it, unadorned of any trimmings. The bread alongside it was a heavy lump, the crust nearly black in colour— coarsely ground, it was a peasants' food. "This is all there is at present. I would go to Bladon or to the Palace itself to get you better if the weather outside were not so foul."

"Why should you go, Blanche?" I asked, shocked. "That is the role of the kitchen staff. Why are the supplies so low? Where is Cook? Is he unwell?"

Blanche licked her lips, looking uneasy. "I have tried to keep it from you, mistress, for I knew you were already consumed with your worries, but a sickness has come to the Tower. A sickness that causes violent vomiting and griping of the bowels. Cook is virtually immobile and his assistants are all affected—over the past day, they have taken to their beds and cannot lift their heads from the bolster! Many of the guards too have fallen down at their stations; thank goodness we have little to fear from old Eleanor these days!"

"And you, are you well?" Fear bit into me, turning my flesh to ice. Outside the Tower, the wind rose, a hoot of unearthly laughter.

"I am fine, my lady," she said, but I noticed that she was pale and that her hands kept clenching, the knuckles white.

"You are ill," I said. "You must go and rest. Tomorrow, we will see who is best able to go and fetch a physician from the Palace."

She bowed her head. "I feel dreadful leaving you alone. I would send Orable to you, but I cannot lie—she has also fallen prey to this dreadful blight."

"Both of you rest," I soothed. "I shall be all right. I am not very hungry anyway. The fire is blazing and the room is warm and I have my Psalter and my romances to read. I am already attired for sleep. Do not fear for me."

Blanche clumped away, hand pressed to her belly in pain, her footsteps heavy on the stairs. I sat in silence, the black bread left untouched before me. I ate the fish; hastily, for my stomach roiled, and then tossed the bread out the window for the birds to devour.

Then I used the little set of steps that allowed me, with my burgeoning size, to mount my bed with ease, and drew the covers over myself. I had intended to read but a sudden weariness descended over me, making my head heavy and my vision blur. I watched as the little taper by my bedside melted away and the fire burned low…and then I slept.

Disorientated, I woke in pitch-darkness. The fire had guttered; the room was icy. How long had I slept? What time was it? No light crept in between gaps in the shutters; night still held sway at the Tower.

Far away, as if in a dream I heard Patch bark. Once, twice, then nothing. He was locked in with the sick serving staff, in his favourite place; no doubt he'd heard a rat or gone for the big piebald Tom-cat that lurked in the kitchens.

Sinking down into my warm covers, I began to drift off again, eager to ward off the pervasive cold that nipped the end of my nose.

And then I heard another sound. Soft footsteps on the stairs. I shifted and turned over, just as my door glided open soundlessly. Despite Henry's orders, it was seldom ever locked these days. Caution had slipped away long ago, familiarity quelling fears.

A dark shadow slid into the room, black against the blackness. Halting, it stood and a shapeless, formless, night-clad head swivelled in my direction. I felt hidden eyes watching, burning into me.

For a moment, I thought it might be the King, arrived late at Woodstock and wishing to surprise me. He had done so before. But an air of menace hung over the room and the sensation of being watched was not a pleasant one.

"Blanche?" I said tremulously, although instinctively I knew the figure was not that of my maid.

A candle flicked to life and was thrust onto the nearby table. I gasped as its light blossomed to reveal the smirking face of a woman. For an awful second I thought it might be Queen Eleanor herself, seeking revenge as Henry had feared she might. But that was a foolish thought—Eleanor was far away at Sarum, locked up with her solitary maid Amaria, by report so reduced in circumstances that she was forced to share a bed with her servant.

Then, as the face swam nearer, I realised it was a familiar one. A face belonging to someone I had not thought of for years. Someone who hated me. Juliana.

I had never learned, nor really cared, what became of her when I sent her from the Tower. I had assumed she lived locally and returned to a family home. I certainly had not expected to see her return to the Tower in this manner…and how did she get in? Years had passed since her dismissal; the guards would never have allowed her access.

"Why are *you* here?" I tried to keep the quiver of fear from my voice. "Have you gone mad? Are you drunk?"

Juliana laughed, tossing back her long brown hair, which hung loose like that of a hoyden, the ends dripping with water where she had passed through the snowy night outside. "Drunk with happiness," she smirked. "I thought this night would never come. A night where I could take my revenge. When the Queen could take her rightful revenge on the little trollop who has brought her so much shame!"

"The Queen!"

"Oh yes." Juliana's eyes glittered; chips of pale ice. "You have heard that she has but one maid, Amaria? What good luck that Amaria happens to be a kinswoman of mine. Eleanor is forbidden to walk free or have discourse with outsiders, but Amaria is not a prisoner, she is guilty of nothing. I am her dear cousin—who would suspect two simple women of concocting a plot to help the Queen? Eleanor has promised many riches if I can rid her of her long-time burden—you, Rosamund Clifford. How could I refuse? I need a job after being thrown out by a harlot no better than she should be." Her upper lip curved in a sneer that gave her a fierce, animalistic look.

"How did you get in here?" Sliding from the bed, I grabbed a robe and wrapped it around my shivering body as I tried to inch away from Juliana. "Why didn't the guards or kitchen servants stop you?"

"One thing at a time, my *Lady*," she said mockingly. "I'll have you know I didn't come through the kitchens. Long ago, I learned the way through the labyrinth." She tapped her chest with obvious pride. "I entered through the tunnel leading into the gardens rather than the one for the servants."

Stunned, I shook my head. "How did you find the way? It was forbidden to you!"

She spat on the floor. "When I...*served* you, I was often bored and went exploring, despite being warned not to. What are rules, if not to be broken? I even followed you and the King when you went there to rut like animals. Always wondered if my knowledge of this place would come in useful one day...after you threw me out, to starve, whore, or die."

She grinned at me, not a friendly smile, more of a leer. I noticed time had not been kind to her; a scar marred her brow and two teeth were gone. "Do you know what I did afterwards, Rosamund? Do you know?"

"No, what did you do?" She was mad; surely, she was mad. I attempted to keep her talking about trivialities while I edged toward the door, determined to scream for Blanche and Orable, even if they must drag themselves from their sickbeds on hands and knees.

"There is an old woman in the village. Old Sully. Everyone hates and fears her. She has a wen on her nose and she feeds a crow. She took me in, as a helpmeet since she's half-blind. I...learned many things from Sully. The art of poisoning for one..."

She cackled like a witch in some dreadful legend. "That has paid off."

My hand rose to cover my mouth as a terrible realisation dawned. "The...the illness affecting my household! Blessed Mary, it is not...you haven't dared..."

"Oh it won't hurt them," said Juliana dismissively. "I have no wish to harm decent, hard-working folk. Only make them sick for a few days, and very sleepy. Too sleepy to check if they really heard the door from the garden open."

"I still I don't understand why the guards allowed you to access any of the tunnels. Did you learn evil magic from that old witch to make you invisible too?" My head was spinning at the enormity of what Juliana had done.

"Handy to have a lover who is one of the guards," Juliana crowed. "Strong in the arm, thick in the head—that's Edgar! He'd do anything for me; I promised that if he let me in we'd be rich! Go to live in London! He persuaded his mates to drink the beer I'd brewed, laced with my potions…and soon they were all hurling, just like the kitchen workers. When they crawled out of sight, too sick to care, he let me pass."

"But a key…you would need a key…"

"I have a key!" She brought out a shining key upon a chain, dangled it triumphantly. "I think you will find Cook is missing something. He is probably too ashamed—and afraid—to mention it. And if you are wondering how I came by it…Well, he was at market in Oxford and I happened to spot him blundering around the fishmongers. A lucky encounter…for me. I picked the fat fool's pocket!"

"What do you plan to do?" My gaze locked upon her, beseeching. I was hardly able to fathom what was happening. The Queen would take her revenge but not as Henry had thought, with soldiers arriving to wrest me from the Bower, but through a jealous woman whose mind had been turned as a product of Henry's own brief lust.

"What do you think?" Juliana said evilly, and from her shabby robes she yanked a long knife with a glimmering handle of bone. "Eleanor wants you gone. I will shed no tears for you either, with your haughty airs and graces. You flung me out in disgrace; my reputation in tatters!"

I doubted anything I did could have made her reputation worse, going by what Blanche had told me after Juliana's departure, but I would not rile her further by saying so. I tried to appeal, even as my terror threatened to overwhelm me and send me into fits of shrieking. "Juliana, you must not contemplate this act! To murder not only another woman but an unborn child as well…What penance could you ever do to atone for such an act?"

"Penance," she laughed. "I care not for all the gabble and gobble of priests, most of whom would have your skirts up in a moment should you let them! Truth be told, as I see it I'd rather get a nice reward on earth, from the Queen, than wait for one in heaven that may never be forthcoming."

She cast me a mocking look. "But fear not, Rosamund. I am not a cruel beast—not like you when you hurled me away like the contents of an old pisspot! I will give you a choice. The dagger…or *this*…" Reaching under her cloak again, she brought out a stoppered flagon and held it on high. "Poison. Not the sleeping draught and emetic I gave the other residents of the Tower but something strong, something lethal…something brimming with monkshood The trouble is, you might take a while to die by that method. The knife would be painful, but far quicker; I used to butcher lambs with my father in Bladon. I know how to slit a throat or strike the heart."

She gave a shrill, mad laugh and suddenly struck out with the knife, sticking the blade into the mattress of my bed. The fabric tore with a loud ripping sound; I realised the madwoman was demonstrating how sharp the blade was.

I let my gaze run over her; whipcord thin, doubtless used to hard work and strong. What chance did I, feeble and pregnant, have against her?

Please God, please God, please God, my voice thundered in my own head but God did not answer this sinner, this carnal woman who had surrendered her virtue too lightly when the time came, who bore beneath her belt a child of sin, for all its royal ancestry…

Juliana had retrieved her knife and was cradling it like a child. I felt the living child beneath my breast move sharply. My head swam. Juliana was mumbling hurtful words that stabbed into me as surely as that honed blade would. "Look at you, full with the fruit of your wicked lusts! Proud of it, are you? Yet what is it but another of the King's many byblows! You do know he has recently added a new brat to his long list of bastards? A son, William, by Ida de Tosney, Duchess of Norfolk?"

I gasped; I could not help myself—it was as if someone had struck me in the belly with a fist. I had supposed there were other women during Henry's long absences, but no direct news had come of any other than the ones I already knew about, and I would not dig for such unwelcome knowledge. But to hear of Ida de Tosney sharing the King's bed—she was of high family indeed, and was even related to me through my mother! Not only that, Juliana said the babe was called William, the same name Henry had told me we would call *our* firstborn son…. *William…*

Juliana's eyes glittered; clearly, she enjoyed tormenting me with the news of Henry's infidelities. "Poor foolish Rosamund," she taunted. "Henry's latest indiscretions are obviously unknown to you. Poor, foolish cow! I suppose you haven't heard the other tales either? That he is bedding his ward, Alais—the French princess who is his son Richard's betrothed? Richard has refused to marry her, so disgusted is he! Some say Henry means to marry her himself, throwing *you* aside, you used up trull."

Mouth open, I gaped, stunned by another, even crueller tale of betrayal…and then Juliana was upon me, the knife cold against my neck. Her breath hit my face, rank, malodorous. "So, which shall it be, King's whore. The dagger or the drink."

"The…the drink…" I croaked, feeling the edge of the knife bite the skin of my throat.

I heard the stopper in the flagon pop, fall to the floor. The knife was whisked away, but as I attempted to dash for safety, my body cumbersome with the child, Juliana kicked out, driving my feet from under me. I fell heavily to the floor and she descended upon me with arms like iron bands, holding me as tightly as she forced the lip of the flagon against my teeth. Cold, vile-tasting liquid rushed into my mouth; I choked, writhed.

"Swallow it! Swallow it!" screamed Juliana, striking me with her fists.

I swallowed, tears streaming down my cheeks, knowing I felt my own death running down my gullet toward my heart, my belly.

Juliana forced me up onto my knees, still pouring her draught of death into my mouth. I choked, gasped; the liquid splashed over my clothes and ran like rivulets of blood across the floor. She loomed over me like a dark angel, her back to the open door of the chamber. "I will watch your end, no matter how long it takes. Then I will return to the Queen with my happy tidings. By tomorrow evening I should be a wealthy woman."

A sudden surge of desperate energy filled me. Fear, anger, hatred, despair flooded my being, even as the deadly monkshood wended its way through my body. "You may have slain me, Juliana…but you will not have the pleasure of watching the love of a King die."

Rising from my knees, staggering as a wave of dizziness washed over me, I struck my enemy with all the force I could muster. Taken unawares, Juliana stumbled backwards, flailing her arms and dropping the flagon of death to smash upon the floor. Encouraged, I struck her again, the heavy rings Henry had given me driving into her face, their rough edges drawing blood. She shrieked and staggered, grasping the ornamented edge of the doorway leading to the stairs, her foot in its worn shoe teetering over the edge. Behind her, shadows danced in the vast stone spiral that led down to the hall floor and the kitchens at the bottom.

I pushed her, my arms trembling with a supreme effort. With a scream, she fell over backwards, turning with arms outflung in an attempt to steady herself, and instead cartwheeling away into the darkness. Crawling, I knelt on the doorsill, watching her fall like a child's discarded doll, bouncing off the adamant walls, limbs twisted and dangling at odd, distorted angles. Striking a stone, her head cricked to one side and an awful, ominous cracking noise reached my ears, and then redness ran over the step and down into the dark. She ceased to move, lay on the step with mouth gaping, eyes wide, reflecting the sullen glow of the guttering torches.

Breath tearing in my lungs, I staggered back from that awful sight, as the first cramps seized my guts and made my legs grow weak.

I must purge! I had learned such from my days with the nuns at Godstow. Running to the privy, I hung myself over the edge of the wooden seat and thrust my fingers down my throat. I vomited and vomited, all the while praying that Blanche would awaken from her drugged slumber and come to find me. She could fetch milk; they said milk could help to dilute ingested poisons.

But no one came, and the pain in my gullet became as sharp as a thousand knives. Weird visions drifted before my eyes. Laying my head on the ground, I commended my own soul to God and waited for death to claim me.

The soft singing of nuns awoke me. Slowly, shakily, I opened my eyes and stared up at a vaulted stone ceiling where carved angels blew trumpets from the dusty corners.

I knew that room! Godstow!

Opening my mouth, I strove to speak. No sound would emerge at first; then a shrill, unnatural squeak filled the chamber. I did not recognise my own voice.

I tried to raise my arm. Nothing. I was weak and felt heavy as if my limbs were wrought of clay. Clay…Was that not another word for a corpse, a hulk devoid of all life?

Gasping in fear, I started to struggle. The linen covers over me twisted like a winding sheet on a cadaver.

"Rosamund, be at peace, be at peace!" The door of the chamber opened and into the chamber swept my old friend Hosanna, followed by the round-faced sister Infirmarer and Prioress Edith. They clustered around my sickbed, pushing me back down onto the pillow and cool, bleached sheets, and Sister Infirmarer felt my brow and gave me a few drops of something to drink from a crystal phial.

"How come I here…" My voice emerged, flat, old, croaking, still a stranger's.

"You were poisoned," said Edith. "Do you remember? Your maid Blanche found you, and Jesu be praised, had the presence of mind to get milk down you to counterbalance the poison. You were then brought here on a litter to be cared for. We were most shocked; for three nights we thought you would surely die. Extreme unction was given to you by the priest."

"Juliana…Juliana did it…for the Queen…" I murmured. I choked a little; drool trailed out the corner of my mouth.

The three nuns glanced at each other and crossed themselves. "You must not speak of the Queen again, Rosamund," said the Prioress sternly. "Such charges would not go well, true or not. As for the girl who attacked you…she is dead."

"She fell…" I gasped.

"God be praised," murmured Hosanna, who received a glare from her superiors.

"My…my baby...?" I strove to touch my belly; it felt flat, shrivelled. Empty.

"I am sorry," said Sister Infirmarer, "but no. There was no hope. It was a miracle you survived; that miracle did not extend to the child."

I fell back, throat constricting with sobs that would not, could not emerge—I had lost the strength to weep.

"You must rest," said Sister Infirmarer. "Whatever has happened is God's will. We will care for you at Godstow, and with Christ's mercy and that of his Blessed Mother, maybe, just maybe, you will recover."

"I want the King...I want Henry to come to me..." I turned my face away from them toward the cold grey wall.

It was spring in England, but there was no spring for me. I was like the last leaf of winter, left dangling and withered on a half-dead tree. My hair had fallen out in clumps in the aftermath of my poisoning, and the scanty remains were gathered beneath a modest hood. I could scarcely eat, for whatever Juliana had mixed with the monkshood had burned my innards. My throat constricted when I attempted to down anything more substantial than gruel, and in the privy I passed blood. I was as weak as an ancient crone and walked only with the aid of a hawthorn cane that Hosanna had brought for me.

And the King, he had not come. Not himself. Only a brief letter that said near to nothing, and an emerald cup. The cup gladdened me, even if his missive did not—emerald was said to counteract most poisons.

So he thought of me. *Thought of me.*

But did not come. (Did he now also think of Alais, plump, nubile, *healthy* Alais, that princess who should have wed his son but was now rumoured to share Henry's bed?)

I walked in the nun's herb garden, leaning on the sturdy shoulder of my friend Hosanna. I pretended to the nuns that I was recovering, but in truth, I was growing weaker rather than stronger. My bones stuck out through my thinning flesh; my skin grew translucent pale.

"You look as though a light glows within you," said Hosanna in wonderment one day, as she guided me through the beds of thyme, lavender and rosemary. "It is almost...holy."

Leaning stiffly, painfully, I plucked a sprig of rosemary—the plant of remembrance. Or should I have plucked rue instead?

"It is growing dark today, Hosanna," I whispered, my ruined voice still a stranger's in my own ears. The poison had wrest that from me as well as my child. "Why is it so dark?"

146

Hosanna's brow furrowed in consternation and she bit her lip. "But...but Rosamund, it is not dark—the sun is shining brightly over Godstow! Can you not feel its warmth?"

"I can only feel the cold...So cold..."

"Let me help you to a seat, Rosamund! You look so strange!"

She guided me to a marble bench where I slumped on the chilled stone, my back pressed against a moss-furred wall. The air, the stone, the seat, my own flesh...All felt so cold, even though the sun was out.

Glancing up, the sky seemed to have taken on the hue of midnight, with the sun a distant, cheerless dot receding into a tunnel—eerily like the path leading through the labyrinth at Woodstock. "Hosanna, hold me, help me." Weakly, I clutched at my friend's chilled fingers, vaguely heard her shouting for assistance as I fell.

High above, on the tower of the priory church, the dimming, shimmering, fading tower, a brief movement caught my attention as I lay weak, breath labouring, upon the ground. Ivy danced in the breeze, its fronds streaming out towards me like a pair of cool, verdant, welcoming arms...

The Green Lady, that myth of my childhood, that fabled sacrifice to love, waved and beckoned, drawing me forward with promises of rest. Promises of eternity where pain was at an end.

I had to resist her lure. If I should take her hand, her green, shining hand, there would be no return.

Then I heard a noise, distracting me from the primal figure clinging to the church tower. Hooves ground upon gravel outside the convent wall; horses neighed and harness jingled. The sounds cut through the perpetual ringing that had assailed my tortured ears since Juliana poisoned me, bringing me hope, that most dear thing, and lightening the shadows that embraced me.

"He's coming," I said, suddenly myself again, suddenly possessed of a great, unbearable joy. I smiled and it seemed white light rose around me in great clouds like the breath of the angels. I could not see the church tower, the Green Lady, Hosanna's tear-splashed face... "Henry, my King, my lover is coming for me. *Henry*..."

148

HISTORICAL NOTES

Rosamund Clifford was a real person and sometime in around 1176, she stepped out of life and into myth. Her story continued to grow and change down the centuries and was particularly favoured by the pre-Raphaelites, who liked to paint images of the innocent maiden caught by the 'wicked queen' within the Bower.

What facts remain about Rosamund? Not many. She was probably born at Clifford Castle on the Welsh Border (remaining only as an overgrown earthwork and a fang of masonry today), and was the daughter of Walter Clifford and Margaret de Tosney, and sister to five siblings. Her exact date of birth is unknown and one author even questioned her name, believing she was really called 'Jane', (which seems unlikely as Jane was not a current name in 12th C England). Certainly, Rosamund was known by that name in her own lifetime, as mentioned in the rude, mocking commentary of Geraldus Cambrensis. It was also apparently the name graven on her tomb, dismantled and moved by the orders of St Hugh of Lincoln.

As a royal mistress, she has received better press than many other royal mistresses, with Queen Eleanor 'taking the blame' and being the antagonist of the story rather than an injured party. Henry II, who was a notable womaniser, seemed to get no blame for any of his actions at all.

The Victorians, in particular, did not like Eleanor—older than Henry, sexually adventurous with no consequences, powerful and politically motivated—this was the kind of women they feared as 'unnatural.' This is where it gets a bit foggy regarding Rosamund's origins and stories start appearing that make her sound much older than she probably was, a childhood contemporary of Henry, who was his first young love. (This is not borne out by chroniclers who mention she died sometime around thirty.)

In reality, Henry and Rosamund probably met at her father's castle in the mid-1160's, when Henry was preparing to move against the Welsh and began their affair around 1165-6. Rosamund was most likely only in her teens, as she would have been married otherwise. The 'first love' myths actually gave rise to later legends that they were married in secret before Henry met Eleanor making Rosamund the 'true' Queen rather than Eleanor. These myths also make her the mother of his two best-known bastards, Geoffrey (later Archbishop of York) and William Longspee; however, records state Geoffrey's mother was a prostitute called Ykenai, and in Longspee's own hand he wrote that his mother was Ida de Tosney, Duchess of Norfolk.

Rosamund's Bower, of course, is a famous part of the story, a fantastical maze or labyrinth near the Palace of Woodstock. Undoubtedly, the maze/labyrinth is only a myth, but there does seem to be traces of ancient buildings in this area, and Rosamund's Well still stands today. Perhaps Henry did build a special house in the vicinity for his mistress.

The poisoning by Queen Eleanor is, of course, mythical Eleanor was in captivity at the time this event was supposed to have taken place. However, *something* happened to Rosamund—her affair with Henry, made public in 1174, ended rather suddenly and she went into Godstow nunnery. She was dead by 1176. What ended their affair? Illness, perhaps…or maybe the fact that there were indeed rampant rumours that Henry intended to marry the French Princess Alais, his own son's betrothed, if Eleanor would grant him an annulment.

In ROSE OF THE WORLD, I have tried to include any known historical detail alongside necessary fictional invention and attempted to follow the actual timeline of real-life events. Occasionally I have moved events a little closer together to keep up the flow. A few of Henry's mistresses who are mentioned may have actually been with him a little later than this period. I also made the flogging he received for his part in Becket's death even more public than it probably was. All medieval poems/songs are real, although my versions of them.

J.P. REEDMAN, FEB 2017

PLACES TO VISIT CONNECTED WITH ROSAMUND CLIFFORD

Godstow Priory. A few miles outside of Oxford, on an islet in the river. Scanty ruins but atmospheric.

Westenhanger Castle, Kent. One tower there is known as Rosamund's Tower. She was said to have met with the King there for secret trysts.

Rosamund's Well, Everswell. Well near Blenheim Palace.

Clifford Castle, Herefordshire. Scanty remains of the border castle where Rosamund was most likely born.

OTHER BOOKS BY J.P. REEDMAN:
RICHARD III:

I, RICHARD PLANTAGENET-Tant Le Desiree Part 1.
The young Duke of Gloucester at Barnet and Tewkesbury. His fights with
George and married to Anne Neville. The Scottish campaigns.

I, RICHARD PLANTAGENET- Loyaulte Me Lie Part 2.
Kingship. The mystery of the Princes. The betrayal of Buckingham and the
Stanleys. The final charge at Bosworth.

Omnibus Edition of I, RICHARD PLANTAGENET CONTAINING BOTH PARTS now available in Kindle and Print. Over 230,000 words!

SACRED KING.
Historical fantasy novella set at the time of Bosworth...and beyond. The afterlife of the King in the twilight realm of faerie...which Richard sees as Purgatory. A tale of hope and redemption, and of the finding of the long-dead King in a Leicester car park. A chance find...or not? The Return of the King.

WHITE ROSES, GOLDEN SUNNES.
Compilation of short stories (156 pages) of stories about Richard III and his family, frequently dealing with Richard's childhood and youth. Includes the tragic tale of his brother Edmund of Rutland.

MEDIEVAL:

MY FAIR LADY - A Story of Eleanor of Provence, Henry III's Lost Queen. First person fiction on the life of this half-forgotten Queen, who was the wife of Henry III, mother to Edward Longshanks...and one time regent of England. Set at the time of the second Barons' Revolt. An Amazon Best Seller in Historical Biographical Fiction and Medieval Historical Romance.

KING ARTHUR/PREHISTORIC:

STONE LORD: The Legend of King Arthur. The Era of Stonehenge.

Britain, 1900 BC, the Great Trilithon at Stonehenge has been unruled for many years. Attackers seeking Britain's tin assail the shores. The shaman known as the Merlin seeks a youth who can draw the Sword from Beneath the stone and unite the warring clans. A retelling of the Arthurian legends with a prehistoric twist. Archaeology and legend combine.

MOON LORD : The Fall of King Arthur.The Ruin of Stonehenge.
Standalone sequel to STONE LORD. Ardhu the Great Chief's illegitimate son Mordraed comes to Kham-El-Ard to claim his birthright. A twisted youth with a face as fair as a god's but bearing a tormented heart, he wreaks terrible vengeance on his hated father by slaying, secretly, his half-brother, the otherworldy young warrior Gal'havad. Power growing, he then seeks to destroy Khor Ghor, the Giant's Dance on the Great Plain.

FANTASY:

BETWEEN THE HORNS: Tales From The Middle Lands.
Collection of humorous fantasy stories for all ages, set in a mythical central European country where each of the towns tries to out perform the others in its celebration of the seasons. A land between the Horn Mountains where giant hares lay eggs, trollocs dwell and the Krampus whips unruly children, where witches control the weather and look for fat boys to eat, and the Erl King rides in bleak midwinter. In the vein of Tim Burton.

MY NAME IS NOT MIDNIGHT
Dystopian fantasy set in a post apocalyptic 70's Canada. A young girl sets out on a quest to fight the religious oppression of the Sestren. In the vein of Philip Pullman.

Printed in Great Britain
by Amazon

60736516R00088